To Love a Runaway

LaJoyce Martin

To Love a Runaway

To Love a Runaway

by LaJoyce Martin

©1989 Word Aflame Press
Hazelwood, MO 63042-2299

Cover Design by Tim Agnew

Cover Art by Art Kirchhoff

All Scripture quotations in this book are from the King James Version of the Bible unless otherwise identified.

Printed in United States of America.

Printed by

Library of Congress Cataloging-in-Publication Data

Martin, LaJoyce, 1937-
    To love a runaway / by LaJoyce Martin.
        p.   cm.
    ISBN 0-932581-42-0
    I. Title.
    PS3563.A72486T64 1989
    813'.54—dc19
                                  88-31620
                                  CIP

Contents

Chapter One

The Leaving of the Last

"Sally's awful moody lately, Henry." Martha's words jabbed through the new periodical Henry held in his hands.

"I declare, Martha. If'n you ain't got som'thin' to worry 'bout, you *invent* som'thin'!" Lowering the farm journal with a patient sigh of resignation, he removed the wire-rimmed monocle from his failing left eye.

"Invent, nuthin'. If'n you was a little more discernin' . . ."

"Martha, of *course* Sally's moody! It's 'er age. She's jest a' unfinished woman yet. She buttoned up 'er schoolin' last year at seventeen year old an' most o' 'er friends've gone off to th' city fer work . . ."

"I'd as lief send 'er into a den o' wild wolves er writhin' rattlers than allow 'er to job as a sody jerk. Henry, 'tain't *decent* fer a young lady. An' I ain't layin'

7

my youngest's name on people's tongues! No siree!"

". . . An' b'sides, Martha, she ain't got no beau."

Martha wiped her flour-dusty hands on her cambric apron and came to stand directly in front of her husband. "She has plenty o' time fer *that*, Henry."

"I was jest tellin' you why she's so moody. Hadn't you wanted my opinion, you shouldn't'a lifted th' subject! You was married a'time you was her age, *an takin' yore moodiness out on me!*"

"Henry Harris!"

"No need Henry Harrisin' me. What you need to do is give th' girl less bridle an' more tether. This phase'll pass off as she gets older an' settleder."

Martha affixed her faded gray eyes, revealing the strain of piloting many children from cradle to maturity, upon her phlegmatic husband. "I think she's got too much slack a'ready, Henry. That may be th' trouble."

"Don't she do 'er share o' th' work 'round here?"

"With 'er hands but not 'er heart."

"Put yoreself in th' girl's stead, Martha." The magazine dropped to the floor, along with the man's dream of a peaceful evening with his publication. "What heart could you muster fer a lonesome place o' forty acre, a lame cow an' molty hens, if'n you was young . . . an' th' purtiest o' th' whole crop o' Harrises?"

"Purty feathers don't make a fine bird . . ."

"Whate'er their feathers, birds is made to fly when flyin' time comes—not to be caged up away from other birds their own kind . . ."

"An' jest what er you suggestin', Henry? That we sell th' place here an' move 'er to th' city where there's medicine shows 'n dance halls 'n all th' bilious devilment?"

Indignation honed her words.

"I ain't suggestin' nuthin'. I'm jest tellin' you why our Sally, th' last o' th' Harrises, is broody. That's th' subject you lifted to disturb my readin' . . ."

"Go back to yore readin' if'n that's what's most important to you, Henry. As if'n she ain't part yor'n an' a joint responsib'lity!"

Before Henry could regroup for a last word, the back screen slammed with a bang, ushering in a flushed Sally, her rebellion ill-concealed. Stray ringlets about her face waged their own insurrection against the imprisoning shovel bonnet, aided by the dampness of her forehead. The smell of spring, stolen from blossoms outdoors, clung to her homespun pinafore.

"Looks like th' hens outdid theirselves today," Henry chortled, surveying the heaping basket of eggs Sally carried.

"They always do on tithe-day. Who started this ridiculous idea, anyhow?" Sally pushed her bonnet back sullenly, looking from Martha to Henry.

"Why, Sally, we've always tithed on ever'thing. An' yore Maw figgered it'd be a passel easier to jest give th' parson all th' eggs ever' tenth day than count 'em out one by one."

"I believe those hens can count."

"They mayhap can't, but th' good Lord shore can. Th' tenth o' ever'thing b'longs to Him an' is extry special . . ." Sally braced herself for the rhetoric she had heard all her life—*Yore th' tenth, Sally, our tithe baby, an' yore special*—willing herself not to hear.

She washed the eggs at the kitchen sink, gazing out the window but seeing nothing of the familiar back-yard vista. What was so "special" about being the last child at home, five years removed from the other nine? They had all made their niche in life—even Robert at rest in the cemetery—leaving her to gather eggs, turn hems, and go to church twice on Sunday.

Her sketchy memory exhumed incidents from the past and converted them to sparkling adventures. For instance, the annual brush arbor meetings were once spirited services of indefinite length conducted by enthusiastic younger evangelists, but now were predictable and ritualistic affairs, administered by a stolid elderly man without charisma. As Pastor Stevens aged, he forgot the needs of the younger generation and settled into his fleece-lined rut. The community's social life, instead of thriving with excitement, was now limited to sewing bees for matrons and barn raisings for neighboring farmers. The monotony of existence seemed to loop a noose about Sally's neck, subjecting her to a choking death of stagnation.

The embryo of a plan had been forming in her mind for weeks. And refusing to uproot it as her conscience urged, she nurtured it. That plan was to leave forever the gray nothingness of Brazos Point, severing the invisible cord. In anticipating her escape, she disciplined her mind to dwell on the advantages of emancipation and to crowd out thoughts of the wound too deep for healing that she knew her leaving would inflict upon her family.

She had awaited the advantages of warm and agreeable weather . . . and now it was here. Her opportunity to slip away would come. Soon.

Martha, sensing Sally's restlessness, sought the harder to rectify the problem, trying mother-like to interest Sally in domestic diversions.

"Let's us make you a new dress, Sally," she offered. "I'll learn you some fancy stitchin'. I noticed th' Mercantile in Th' Springs had in some new ribbon in all sorts o' purty colors. It set my fingers to itchin'."

Sally raised her eyebrows, but said nothing.

"Ain't you hankerin' fer a flattersome garment?"

"There's nowhere to wear it." Sally's voice was flat.

"To church."

"I'm sure Pastor Stevens would be unimpressed."

Martha tried again. "Crocheted collars er in high style. You want that I learn you to crochet?"

"No, I'm . . . I'm afraid sitting for hours poking a needle at thread would only bore me the worse. Maybe when I'm older . . ."

Meeting failure at every crossroad, Martha approached Henry a second time in desperation with a half-compromise. "Henry, yore right 'bout Sally needin' an outin' where there's other birds o' 'er kind. I been thinkin' we'd best plan a trip into Th' Springs come Saturd'y an' let 'er see some o' 'er friends what works there. I said I'd ne'er let 'er 'sociate with that flapperish granddaughter o' Myrt's what works as a sody jerk, but havin' a sody at th' drug store t'gether might not taint Sally too much."

"You speakin' o' Molly Rushing, Martha?"

"Yessir."

"She don't seem flapperish to me."

"I wouldn't 'spect you to be judgmental along them lines, Henry. How does my idee strike you?"

"Fine. Fine. Would it be jest you an' me an' Sally?"

"No. I thought on askin' Sarah an' Hank an' their'n

11

to go along fer th' merryment like old times when we took a wagonload to town a Saturd'y. We could mayhap even picnic like o' yore. Anyways, Sarah's been wantin' to go fer a galavant an' look fer some linsey-woolsey."

"You talkin' 'bout th' Saturd'y next?"

"Will that misput you?"

"Nary a tall. We'll need to leave right early so's to have th' whole o' th' day fer funnin'."

Martha fell to scheming the airin', as she called it, with a will, including a basket lunch of Brobdingnagian proportions. Sally's silent brooding remained unaltered, but Martha's preoccupation with her plans (a surprise for Sally) diminished its import in her own mind.

On Friday night, Martha, wreathed in smiles and cheerfulness, bade Sally good night with her announcement. "Papa's takin' us an' Sarah's fam'ly all into town tomorra, Sally. We'll like as not haunt th' ice cream parlor. You'll mayhap get to see Molly an' sody with 'er. I'll call you at daybust."

Sally saw the chance she sought. "I . . . I believe I'll stay home tomorrow, Mama."

Martha was puzzled, baffled. "I'm takin' a picnic an' all . . ."

"You can leave me some of the food, please, for my lunch. I don't . . . quite feel like making the trip."

"Sally, are you ill?"

"Not . . . really."

"I'll get you some physic an' you'll be feelin' like goin' when you wake, I'm shore." Martha brought the medicine, little knowing it would go out the window.

But when morning pushed the sun up, Sally still resisted Martha's urgings to join the family excursion.

"Then I'll stay with you, Sally. I shain't leave you ailin'."

"Of course you must go, Mama," urged Sally, almost frantically. "Sarah's children will be disappointed if Grandy isn't along. No need worrying about me. This little ole sicky feeling won't last long. I'll feel better before nightfall."

Martha hesitated.

"Bring me back some blue satin ribbon if the Mercantile has any," Sally hurried on amiably. "And tell Molly I send my greetings." Sally's voice actually carried a note of gladness, misinterpreted by Martha, who took the false encouragement as a good sign.

Scarcely waiting for the wagon to rattle out of the yard, Sally flung back the thin, hand-tacked quilt that covered her and prepared for her flight. Her gripsack had been carefully packed for many days, and now all she needed was the lunch Martha left on the kitchen table.

This was simply too good to be true . . . and too easy. The fried chicken, baked yam, biscuits, and cake would last her for two or three days.

The decision to leave a note for Martha caused momentary chagrin. As she picked up the writing tablet, her hands shook and she sensed that her resolve would desert her unless she hurried away. So she dropped the tablet, hastily picked up her baggage, and headed for the river without a backward glance, picking her way through the heavy fretwork of grapevines that hung from the trees.

Every detail of her escape had been worked out in the inner chambers of her mind, and now she followed the mental map she had drawn. The flat-bottom boat that

William had built, held in custody by a hemp rope fastened to a giant cottonwood tree, awaited her. "I'll untie you and we'll both be free," she murmured, not daring to allow her body to make the U-turn her timorous heart dictated.

Past the launching of the boat downstream, Sally's destination was uncharted, unrehearsed. She knew that there were towns all along the river and hoped that she might find ready employment—and a boarding house—in one of these ports. Her plan was to prolong her aquatic journey as long as her food supply and her strength would sustain her, putting as much distance as possible between her and the temptation to return to the community of her beginnings.

Hardly had the Harris wagon swung onto the main road leading past Sarah's cabin until Martha spoke up. "It's been many a day since I seen Sally so heartened, Henry. Course we'll miss 'er on this trip, an' I hated worse'n anything to leave 'er b'hind with 'er puny, but it seemed to make 'er happy that I'd bring 'er back some purty ribbon."

"Jest remember, Martha, Sally's eighteen now, an' unless'n somethin' changes, we won't keep 'er content fer long."

But even Henry's prediction failed to daunt Martha's spirits, and she smiled on, never dreaming that every throbbing moment carried Sally farther from hearth and home.

Chapter Two

Launched

*"H*ere, Patches!"

Jay Walls lay on his back in the creek bank's soft grass, using his small knapsack for a pillow and lulled to drowsiness by the fluid concert of the river and the mid-morning sun. A stubble of a beard, three days old, worried his thin face.

In a bounding leap, the dog was at his side, searching his face with intelligent, questioning eyes. Jay sat up stiffly, patting the shaggy head. "Just wanted to know where you were, old boy. It's just me and you against the world. We've got to stick together." Patches thumped his ragged tail in joyful response.

"And you've been through a patch of beggar's-lice! Here, let me see what I can do about picking the stickers out."

A dull gnawing in the pit of his stomach reminded

Jay that he had eaten nothing since daybreak. His breakfast consisted of a handful of early summer grapes and a small fish broiled on the coals of his campfire. Using his wash-faded shirt for a seine served two purposes: to cleanse the shirt and to provide food. Besides, when he put it back on wet, it was cool.

He figured he had covered less than sixty miles since he left Dublin, the last place his money afforded him the luxury of a roof over his head. Poor time. But his feet wallowed about badly in the stiff leather boots, two sizes too big, causing angry blisters on his heels and the tops of his toes and making travel slow and arduous.

In spite of his echoing memory—or perhaps to drown it out—he whistled a tune. Whistling seemed to calm the rolling turmoil in his mind, fill the void of a lonely heart, and ease the throbbing ache of homelessness. He wasn't the world's best whistler, but he considered himself better than average in the art; his grandmother always loved to hear him whistle about the cottage.

The disconnected tatters of song he warbled eventually fell into a meaningful pattern of rhythm and verse. Upon conscious pondering, he recognized the song his soul played. It was an old church hymn his grandmother favored. *Like a shepherd, Thou wilt lead me. . . .* How ironic. To where? he mused.

Patches raised his ears to fervid alertness, his nose elevated. Jay looked around, then spoke gently. "It's nothing, boy. Just a river bass doing his daily acrobatics." The dog's head went down on his paws, his soft, sad eyes studying his master.

"I can't figure for the life of me, Patches, what that lone girl was doing floating down the river alone . . ."

Jay's mind somersaulted back past the starry night to yesterday. Approaching the railroad trestle, he had seen her and slipped into the brush so as not to disturb or frighten her. He had seen no houses, no village, no signs of civilization for an hour or more.

She hugged the shoreline for shade from the relentless sun, with the river spreading its silver sheet beyond her. The beams of light filtering through the overhanging trees caught her tangle of golden hair, and a wisp of it blew across her forehead. Running her delicate fingers through the soft tresses, she settled it into a befitting frame for her beautiful face.

Once she looked up anxiously, almost prayerfully, making Jay want to step from his seclusion and safeguard her lest an unseen evil claim her. She seemed so young and fragile.

"No, I can't figure it, Patches. She wasn't fishing. She had no pole or bait or stringer. Anyhow, she wasn't dressed for fishing. Folks just don't fish in pretty clothes like that. Why, she was too neat and clean to even touch a smelly fish!"

Patches blinked his serious eyes, which still rested on his master.

"It wasn't a pleasure ride, either, Patches. Not in a crude, flat-bottom boat like that. No, she had a purpose . . ."

Jay fell silent, but his thoughts surfaced again. "Grandma would have called her dress a Sunday-go-to-meetin' tog. It was starched and ironed proper, too. She couldn't have worn anything that would have done her rosy complexion up prettier than that pale blue, almost the color of the sky up yonder. You know, Patches, I've

17

never had the leave to find a bonnie, but if I had one, I wouldn't mind her looking like that . . ."

Jay shook his head. "She was no river bum or waif. That was evident. Too refined for that. She was a lady. Yep, a real lady. I'd say she wasn't from an exactly poor family, either. If she has a family, that is . . ."

Patches stretched and yawned.

"It's sure a puzzle. I couldn't see the delicate features of her face for the shade, but she appeared a little nervous. No, not nervous, Patches, but . . . a little worried.

"What time was it we saw her, old buddy? Must have been near noon. The trees shadowed shallow, driving her close to the bank."

Jay frowned, trying to recall every detail of the strange scene that was etched on his mind like a painting on canvas.

"I *did* really see her, didn't I, Patches? I didn't just imagine it all, did I?"

Patches twitched his ears only slightly and took a long, deep breath suggesting boredom.

"You ready to go, boy?"

Patches gave a short, sharp bark.

"Guess we'd best push some more miles under our feet."

Jay tried to stand, but a pain shot up his leg. He removed his boot and found the blood-soaked worsted sock bonded to his heel.

"Guess I'd better get to the water and soak this sock off before we travel on," he told the dog. "Pardon the delay."

Patches followed him down the embankment, lowering his nose and lapping from the clear river.

18

Jay sat on the short shelf, dangling his feet in the cool current and looking about him. Every little wavelet sparkled like a diamond. To his right, an overarched foot trail led away from the stream bed, resembling a tunnel framed in greenery. To the left stood a giant cottonwood, scarred by an old lightning injury. Its branches of green and silver foliage reached toward the river. He looked at it, then looked again.

"Why, Patches, look there. That old tree has a piece of rope tied around it. And the end of the hemp is still paralyzed in its twisted shape where a knot used to be. Hasn't been undone long."

Patches looked in the direction Jay pointed.

"Must have been a boat put in here . . ."

Patches sat on his tail and scratched his ear with his hind leg.

"Patches!"

Patches stopped his vigorous scratching.

"Do you suppose that girl we saw launched from here? See, she couldn't have untied the rope at the tree without skinning up those pretty little hands. There was a knot farther on down the rope that she managed to get loose."

Jay hobbled toward the tree, temporarily forgetting his foot-soaking task. "Yep, Patches!" excitement saturated his voice. "Here's her footprints right here in the mud. Aren't they tiny ones? Just think, she stood in this very spot . . ."

A pang in his foot reminded him of his mission, and he continued his mulling with the wound again submerged.

"I guess we'll never know who she was or where she was going, old boy. And I expect it's none of our business anyhow. I'd be too poor to win the hand of a fancy thing like that. It's just wishful thinking.

"It sure makes a fellow feel strange, though, seeing a lady helpless on the high tide. You have to keep your mind off what could happen to her. Not all the world is pretty, and not everybody is friendly. We'll just have to pray God to take care of her, since it didn't fall our privilege to do it for Him."

Jay pulled his ailing foot from the water, rolling the sock down carefully, coaxing the fabric from the skin to which it clung doggedly. He gritted his teeth and gave it a quick jerk. The blister on his heel had burst, and the galled red sore seeped with whitish matter.

"Rotten luck, Patches." Jay shook his head. "Infection setting in. You'd best run along and fetch you a rabbit to lunch on. It looks like we'll be here for a day or two yet."

Chapter Three

Laid Up

*T*he snap of a twig brought a low growl from deep in Patches' throat.

"What is it, boy?" Jay motioned the dog close to his side as a man with a battered hat, looking as startled as himself, stepped into the clearing. Jay stared at him, speechless.

Patches awaited Jay's orders, and seeing the dog, the man stopped in deathlike stillness, advancing no farther.

"Beggin' yore pardon fer disturbin' you," the man apologized, his weary brown eyes refusing to smile with the rest of his face. "I was searchin' fer a lost animal o' mine."

"I don't expect I'm woolly enough to be the one you're looking for—yet," laughed Jay, stroking his sticky whiskers. "But could I be of help to you in hunting?" He reached for his boot but winced when the raw place on his heel touched the callous leather, which was pitiless of the injury.

The man was silent, obviously weaving a story from the fabric of the scene he saw in a glance. The blackened fire pit, the crudely tied pack, and the blood-soaked sock worn threadbare in places told their tale well. This harmless-looking young man, somewhere in his twenties, had covered more than a few miles in a relatively short time.

"Guess you hain't seen a' old brindle-colored cow kinda givin' to 'er left front foot since you been here, have you?"

The boyish grin split Jay's face. "You almost described me! Only it's my right foot . . . No, sir. I've been camped right here since last night and haven't seen or heard any animals."

"Traveled a fer piece?"

"Yes, sir. I was aiming on taking up again today, but sore feet slowed me down. I'm not making very good time."

"Goin' someplace in partic'lar?" The question was kind, neither prying nor ill-meant.

"I . . . Yes, I heard that there were a couple of new railroad shops just put in somewhere in central Texas. I'm looking for work."

"Warn't there no railroads where it is you traveled from?" Again the query carried no malignity.

"I could have found railroad work aplenty along the way, but I wanted to locate in a town with a college where I could hope to educate myself on the side while I work."

"You ain't a runaway er you?"

"No, sir. I have no family. My blessed old grandmother who reared me died last month . . ."

"What's your name, chap?"

"Spurgeon Jay Walls. Grandma called me Spurgeon, but my peers called me Jay. Except for one or two who insisted on inventing a nickname. And this is my friend, Patches." Jay jerked his thumb toward the dog.

"I'm Henry Harris, Spurgeon. Pleased to meet you. I think we have jest th' town you might be lookin' fer a hand's turn away. Railroad shops an' a nice academy. My son went there an' took elocution."

"Thank you, Mr. Harris. I'll check it out just as soon as my foot will let me travel. I may have to be here for a day or two. Am I, by chance, trespassing on someone's private property?"

"Oh, there's no problem with that. I'm Indian-natured enough to believe it's all God's land by rights, nohow. If'n a fellow pilgrim has need o' it, I say he's mighty welcome to its use."

Henry paused, appraising Jay, his sluggish mind trying to formulate a solution to the young man's dilemma. How would Martha react to a total stranger in the house on the heels of her fresh grief? *Dare I risk it?* he asked himself.

"I'm in desperate need o' a farmhand fer a few days durin' th' summer rush if'n you'd be innerested in workin' abit afore you move on . . ."

Jay looked at his feet. "I'm in no condition to help you right now, Mr. Harris. I could lend you a hand when these blisters get over."

"Boots too tight?"

"Too loose."

Henry shifted from one foot to the other. "You look

all warshed up, chap. Tell you what. You stay put right here an' rest while I go a'scoutin' fer that cow, an' I'll swing back by in a couple o' hours er so an' we'll go up to th' house."

Henry's motive for leaving the young man was twofold: to give the fellow a chance to make his break if he didn't really want the job and to "warn" Martha that he was bringing someone for lunch. A mighty hungry-looking someone.

Martha fussed predictably. "Henry, what d'ya mean draggin' up a stray fer me to have to cook fer when my heart is heavy as pure granite t'day?"

"He looks famished, Martha. An' th' poor boy ain't got no kith ner kin nowhere. An' b'sides his foot don't look no good a tall to me. Hit's all festered an' corrupted. He'll be right there lackin' nourishment an' nought but a sky fer a roof, if'n I don't bring 'im here. He might even die. What if'n it was one of yor'n, Martha? What if'n it was . . ." Henry bit off the name of Martha's youngest just before it escaped his lips.

Martha sighed heavily, but Henry knew he had won. Behind her barrage of complaints hid a tender maternal heart.

Henry found Jay asleep but Patches on vigilant guard. The dog nudged his master awake.

"Did you find the cow, Mr. Harris?" Jay asked, stifling a yawn.

"I found 'er, all right. She never meanders fer, but insists in playin' hide an' seek with me now an' then. She'd prob'ly a'come home of 'er own come nightfall, but Martha gits to frettin' o'er her. Th' ole milker's been in th' family many a year, an' Martha's afeared she'll wander off an' mayhap stumble an' git down."

"I see."

"Can you make it up to th' house?" Henry held a pair of soft doeskin moccasins in his hand. "Here. Try these'ns on those smartin' feet."

"Mr. Harris . . . you're very generous and I thank you, but I guess I'd best stay out here."

"You look like you could use some hot grub, an' my wife's fixin' up a meal . . ."

"I'm afraid I couldn't leave my dog. It's just me and him against the world. And you might not feel disposed to have Patches around your place."

"Would he have to stay in th' house with you?"

"Oh, no, sir! Patches is no pampered house dog!"

"Then he's welcome as th' bluebonnets o' spring to fetch 'imself a lodgin' under th' front stoop. Martha's been afrettin' 'bout throwin' out scraps an' nuthin' to eat 'um."

At the farmhouse, Henry watched Jay, in his brave effort to hide his suffering, extract Martha's motherly sympathy. She bustled about, her eyes still swollen from an entire night of crying over Sally, doing what she could to make the young man comfortable.

"We'd best soak that foot in Epsom salt," she said after they had eaten, and Henry wondered if she was talking to herself, him, or to Jay.

She stationed her patient in a stuffed parlor chair with antimacassar-covered arms. "Henry said you'd no folks a tall," she said, matter-of-factly.

"That's right, Mrs. Harris."

"Yore maw an' paw both dead?"

"My mother died shortly after I was born, and I know absolutely nothing of my father. My grandmother, who reared me, never mentioned him and hedged my questioning. Grandmother died a month ago after a dozen years of ill health, at the age of sixty-nine. I . . . miss her."

"She left no home to you?"

"No, ma'am. We had to sell everything but the clothes on our backs to buy her medicines. And still it wasn't enough. I worked at odd jobs so as to be with her and care for her as much as possible. She was a complete invalid the last few months of her life."

"Are you a Christian, Spurgeon?"

"Yes, ma'am. It worried me a lot about not having a natural father until I found my . . . Heavenly Father."

"You got a good Christian name."

"My friends called me by my middle name, but Grandma called me by my first name."

"What would you lief we call you?"

"Jay'll be fine. It's shorter and easier."

"You must be 'bout th' age o' my William."

"I'll soon be twenty-five."

"We raised six boys to grown-ups an' a seventh partway," smiled Henry. "An' we raised three girls o' our own an' a niece o' mine till her untimely death. Th' last o' our brood left . . . recently." A stabbing pain seemed to catch away his breath, cutting short further words.

"It's mighty lonely 'round here, jest Paw an' me," Martha spoke with downcast mien. "We're mighty glad you come along, partic'lar today, so our house won't echo so empty t'night."

"It's kind of you to offer such open hospitality, with me a stranger and all."

"I'm shore yore honest an' upright. Anyhow yore story rings true as gold. Henry's a purty good jedge o' character." Henry gave her a quizzical look; it had not been a week since she had labeled him a poor one!

"You say you have a large family, Mrs. Harris?"

Martha padded away to the bureau, bringing back the bulky photograph album, pulling a stool close to the armchair that encased Jay.

"Joseph's our firstborn," she began, opening the book with pride. "He an' Amy lives in th' Territory o' New Mexico with their three childern a'named Davy, Jimmy, an' Josie. They git to come home on th' pullman onct a year, usually on Thanksgivin'. That's when *all* our young uns gather home . . ." Martha stopped abruptly, her troubled eyes filling like lakes threatening to overflow their banks.

"Joseph drove a stagecoach way back yonder afore th' railroads got strung out good," continued Henry hastily. "They been after us fer ten year to come out on a pleasure jaunt an' see their part o' th' country. I hear they ain't much out there but sagebrush an' cactus an' sandhills. It's a mighty fer piece, too. But now that it's jest me an' Maw . . ." Here Henry stopped and turned his head away.

"Our next in line was Matthew." Martha regained her composure.

"He's th' one I tole you what went to college in Th' Springs an' took th' lessons in public speakin'. Wanted to better 'isself to be a preacher," interjected Henry.

"He married th' daughter o' our parson, Brother Stevens. Her name is Pauline, an' they have a little tow-headed boy named Steven, Matthew's very spirit an' image. Matthew travels an' preaches a lot. He ain't got no set place fer services, though they keep a lodgin' up in Th' Springs. He onct had a permanent church, but he got to feelin' God wanted him to go 'round to other places."

"Then there's Sarah. She lives jest down th' road an' acrost. She eloped an' married Hank Gibson, th' neighbor boy, when she was scarce sixteen. But she got 'erself a good un!"

"*He* got a good un," corrected Henry.

"They have four childern an' one in th' cemetery aneath th' Gibson headstone."

"Martha, let's not bore th' man with our family history . . ." Henry objected.

"Oh, let her go on, please, Mr. Harris. I'm very much interested. I often regretted that I was an only child. Large families fascinate me."

"Next after Sarah was our Robert. We didn't get to keep him but thirteen years. He met his death in a accident in town. Horse runaway. He's laid to rest in th' churchyard in a Harris plot. I tho't th' ache o' him would never ever go away. But I b'lieve some things hurt worser than death . . ."

"Turn th' page, Martha . . ."

"After Robert is William, th' one nigh yore age. He's strong as th' oak tree an' took up th' trade o' smithy with his hard an' sinewy hands. He has 'is own shop in Cleburne."

"Is he married?"

"Oh, yes. Married five year ago. Th' neighbor girl, Nellie Gibson. He laughs now that he used to dip 'er pigtail in th' inkwell at school. So fer, they hain't got no childern. You'll like William. *Ever'body* likes William.

"Then there is Dessie. Dessie's husband moved 'er a long way off to a place called Limestone Gap so he could work in th' quarries. We didn't feel good 'bout 'em leavin'.

28

She buried 'er first husband there after a rock fell on 'is head on th' job. Left 'er with a fetchin' baby girl named Becky. She married agin 'bout two year ago. Her new husband is a school superintendent turned preacher an' they got a nice, growin' church in th' Gap. Dessie was always religious-turned."

Martha hesitated, as if realizing she wove in too much detail. "Then we had twin boys."

"That was when President Arthur was in office," Henry spoke up. "We favored th' president so much we named th' twins Chester an' Alan to honor 'im."

"Th' boys was th' ones honored, Henry."

"An' a year later we had another boy an' named 'im Arthur so's we'd have th' whole president."

Jay laughed. "Did the president take a wife?"

"Two-thirds o' him did!" grinned Henry. "Chester wed a girl he met off up in Fort Worth where he was workin' fer th' city puttin' down bricks fer th' streets. She's been here two Thanksgiving's. We ain't right well acquainted with 'er yet."

"Arthur jumped th' broom last year," picked up Martha. "He married th' mayor's daughter, Lucy, up at th' Gap where Dessie an' Nathan lives. Alan's still single, but he's up at th' capital in some kind o' government work. He's military minded. Went to school so many years, there warn't nuthin' else to learn!"

Martha broke off, unwilling to go farther. Jay knew that the last and youngest had not been discussed. The last had purposely been left out. He wisely said nothing.

If I've counted right, the last would be a girl.

Chapter Four

A Place to Dock

"Why, it's a girl, Monroe! A mermaid! I never believed there was such a creature, but here she is."

The alien voice, hard and uncultured, reached Sally's ears, awakening her with a start. *Where am I?*

Two leering men peered at her from the rushes on the steep bank. "Do we use a hook, a seine, or a net to capture her?"

"I dunno. Never heard of one being captured. But she's mine. I seen her first!"

"Maybe we could divide her up between us." Raucous laughs, punctuated by oaths, poured from their vile lips.

Sally looked about wildly. A volcanic shudder ripped through her body. Terror held her in its throes; her heart filled with dread. Death by drowning would be preferable to falling into the hands of these uncouth characters! For an instant, she contemplated jumping overboard.

She had tied her tiny raft to a sapling in a protected cove on the moonless night to grant her body the rest it demanded, and she had wished for the thin quilt she left at home to shield her from the industrious mosquitoes. Thinking herself quite safe and hidden, she immediately fell into an exhausted sleep on the undulant river. Now, miles from home, she faced a new day and a danger her sheltered life had kept her from anticipating.

She sent up a desperate prayer, a source of assistance she shamefully admitted to neglecting since her decision to chart her own course in life. And then, as if directed by a power outside herself, she moved to the front of the boat and began untying the rope from the helm.

"She's gonna loose the thing and get away, Monroe! Quick, we gotta do something . . ."

The final knot stubbornly refused to budge under Sally's fumbling fingers.

"Jump in and hold the boat!"

"And go to work all wet?"

"*Work?*" The roguish man with small, narrow eyes and colorless lashes drew his timepiece from his watch fob and swore. "We're almost late now, Sarge! We gotta hustle and get to them docks or get ourselves fired. No mermaid is worth me losing my job over. My old lady'll have my scalp if I come home without a paycheck."

A shop whistle sounded loud and long in the distance. The two squalid men scrambled through the salt cedars and disappeared.

Sally's heart thumped on violently; even the reflection of her disheveled hair in the water frightened her. She dug clumsily into her handbag for her toiletry to smooth her askew locks, her hands shaking so badly that she almost dropped her comb into the river. Exposure and fatigue had levied an outrageous toll on her sensitive nerves.

I'll stop at the next waterfront city and look for lodging and work, she pledged to herself, easing her craft into the lazy current. In vain she wished for wind to hasten her journey.

The sun's reflection upon the clear water burned Sally's eyes. An insect bite on her hand festered. The whalebone waistband of her petticoat gouged her ribs.

Minutes ballooned into hours, expanded by the journey's miseries. Presently she passed the docks where Monroe and Sarge rolled greasy, blackened barrels up a splintery ramp. The burlier of the two had shed his shirt, and his hard-muscled shoulders were bronzed with sunburn. He stopped and gawked. "Look, Sarge! There goes our mermaid! And prettier than ever in the sunlight, too! She has *gold* hair . . ."

Sally gripped the oar as if for comfort and rowed frantically.

The place she disembarked several hours later was known as Fort Fisher, an abandoned fortress built as protection against the Indians, around which a busy town crawled out like the fingers of a spreading ivy. The bravado, born of rebellion, that she felt two days earlier left her stranded now in an unfamiliar world of quest for mere survival.

She picked up her gripsack, her spirit bent but not broken, and set out to find lodging. On and on she walked, past bales of cotton waiting to be shipped, a livery stable that smelled of old leather, dust, and sweaty horses, and a blacksmith shop with its ringing hammer and flying sparks.

The general store prefaced a row of bawdy saloons, tossing out their tinny music. Sally crossed the street to avoid any patrons that might emerge from their darkened doorways. The bank and attorney's office occupied the next block.

Yet another street farther south, she deliberated in front of the city hotel, shifting her baggage from her right hand to her left, wondering whether to inquire after a room in these quarters. Her body begged respite; the sooner she found lodging, the better.

An ill-assorted group of idlers lounged in the hotel's front lobby, squinting from their cosmos of pipe smoke. Its dingy interior seemed to reach out to her with evil intent. A pale gas light gave the only ray of light in the entire funereal atmosphere.

When one of the loafers stumbled to the door on unsteady feet, almost tripping over his moth-pocked trouser cuffs, Sally goaded her tired body on down the uneven board sidewalk. The railway station loomed next, and the confused girl entered its welcomed shelter and sat for a long while trying to sort her thoughts.

The railway clerk periodically glanced over his spectacles at her, mildly inquisitive, as his shuffling steps thudded on the oiled hardwood floor, taking him about his work. Her attention was drawn to the ceaseless clicking of the telegraph, which at first she found interesting, then boring, and finally irritating as it picked relentlessly at her subconscious mind.

At length, Sally felt that the gentleman's gaze demanded some sort of action on her part, so she stepped to the window and inquired in a timorous voice, "Sir, when does the next train depart for The Springs?"

"You mean Walnut Springs?"

"I . . . suppose so. We always just called it The Springs."

"Railroad town west of Meridian?"

"Yes, sir."

The man checked a cardboard schedule tacked on the plank wall and answered in telegram conciseness. "Next westbound leaves in two hours."

Almost . . . almost Sally decided to board the train back to the comforts of her girlhood home . . . back where logic told her she belonged. But discontent had not yet worked itself out.

"Thank you."

"Need a ticket, ma'am?"

"Not . . . today."

Sally turned onto an angled side street and walked east from the depot where the town thinned from business to residential. Sandwiched between these two worlds, she found a gray clapboard boarding house onto which many appendages had been added over the years, disfiguring the whole. The weather-cracked "Rooms for Rent" sign implored fresh lettering, and the faded "Five Dollars per Week" was hardly legible.

The ridiculously high figure astounded Sally, who had had little experience in financial matters. Why, her entire purse consisted of only eight dollars, which she had supposed would be adequate for an indefinite length of time!

In spite of her consternation, she pulled the string that jingled the bell for the proprietor, not knowing what else to do, dreading the ordeal of renting a room.

"You need a chamber?" The immense puffy-faced

woman who answered the summons fixed her near-sighted eyes on Sally's travel case.

Sally lifted her small chin haughtily. "I . . . is this the only place in town that takes boarders, ma'am?"

"By no means, miss," the owner said snappishly. "There are four others. But this is the best, cleanest, and you can eat all you want. I only got three rooms to let. I stay full up most of the time. I can table twice as many as I let, though."

"Are the others so . . . expensive?"

"I wouldn't know that." Spoken icily.

"Are . . . the others in this vicinity?"

"No, Miss, they're not. The others are farther south, across the railroad tracks. Full of lice and mice and boozers."

Sally felt a queamish sensation begin in the pit of her stomach. "I'll take a room . . . for one week, please."

"I require full payment in advance, plus a four-bit deposit which you get back when you check out proper-ly." There was a hard edge to her voice.

"Yes, ma'am." Sally dipped into her handbag for the roll of bills, removing five and consulting her change purse for the half dollar.

"Follow me." Squandering no words, the hefty pro-prietress led her to a small back room, stifling hot and scantily furnished. "Put your name on this card and bring it down to dinner at six. My name's Gordon." She pulled a wrinkled notesheet from her pocket and handed it to Sally, then took her leave without further conversation.

Sally looked about the pitiful excuse for a bedroom, begrudging her five-dollar fee, but she promptly remem-bered the lice-and-mice reference made by Mrs. Gordon.

She set her bag on the floor and sank wearily onto the hard gray cot. *How rash I was to leave a comfortable . . .* She stopped the thought by determined effort. *I'm eighteen now and no baby!*

Did Mrs. Gordon say *clean?* Dirt had collected on the baseboards, in the corners, on the windowsill. The room reeked with the scent of old shoes and unwashed spittoons.

Sally pulled herself up woodenly, willing her uncooperative arms to the task of unpacking. As she opened the gripsack, a whiff of sachet—a home smell—brought a keen pang of wistfulness. She fought it away. The tiny bureau-washstand, made of cheap pine and sorely needing a facelift of fresh paint, groaned rheumatically as she tugged on the stubborn drawer.

The tiny chipped washbowl poorly substituted for the great bowl and ewer set she had had in her own sleeping room on the farm. She caught her reflection in a narrow-framed, cloudy mirror with a crack across the bottom that was supported by square, rusty nails. The distorted view shocked her.

Dingy flowered wallpaper of ancient design had long overlived its usefulness. Two tattered space rugs, faded and soiled, imprisoned the odors of stale food.

Quickly Sally yielded her personal belongings to the depressingly cramped quarters before the threatening tears could fall. Her jangled mind lost its tussle with raw reality. This wretched dwelling would have to do until she could find a good job and earn some money.

The paper Mrs. Gordon gave her fluttered to the floor; she picked it up and toyed with it. She dare not register under her real name. No one must find her in this hovel!

But to register under any other name would be deceit, a sin her father abhorred.

She walked to the small uncurtained and unwashed window overlooking an alley, opened it, and gazed out, pondering the problem. The wind, blowing from just the right direction, brought the stench of ill-smelling refuse to her nostrils. A spindly chicken pecked through a collection of debris in hopes of finding a grain of nourishment. Before her mind could turn the scene to a simile, she jerked away from the window with smarting eyes. As a compromise, she renamed herself Harriet, not quite willing to relinquish all the familiar syllables of her ancestry and telling herself she was not altogether dishonest.

When she gave the identification sheet to Mrs. Gordon at the lard-soaked, ill-cooked meal, the woman studied Sally critically. "Harriet, have you anyone we can contact in case of illness or emergency?"

Sally hesitated. "No, ma'am."

"Then if you should die, we will turn your remains over to the county for a pauper's burial in an unmarked grave. Is this understood?" Mrs. Gordon, obviously experienced in handling like situations, knew where to strike her victims.

Sally blanched. "Yes, ma'am."

A mist lay thick in the cove that night, eclipsing the moon and blanketing the area in its heavy cocoon. Only the flickering light of the street lamp punctured the blackness. Sounds of the strange city ripped jagged holes in Sally's sleep, while the rocklike cot and lumpy flock pillow added to her general discomfort.

Sometime after midnight, a clanging fire wagon

brought a new horror to her sick mind and body. What if the boarding house caught fire? Her tortured mind kept repeating like a cylinder recording, *Pauper's burial . . . unmarked grave . . .* She shook with a feverish chill, and her lips burned.

Before the light of morning, she had made a momentous decision. The perception of the prodigal son became her own. Why suffer thus in a disheveled tenement house when a comfortable room was hers for the returning?

Her driving ambition was to get well enough to board the westbound train and go home.

Chapter Five

A Familiar Room

"You'd best show Jay to 'is room, Martha. He's all awash." Held in the chair's comforting embrace, Jay's head doddered and he stifled a yawn.

"We got rooms aplenty since the younguns er all gone. I guess you can have yer choice." Martha gave Jay a motherly smile set in a background of sorrow.

"You'll find that I'm not a bit particular, Mrs. Harris. This chair seems like heaven's cloud to me."

"But a bed'll seem more heaven," she laughed.

"Put 'im in th' south front bedroom, Martha. That's th' coolest in summer an' most comfort'ble furnished b'sides."

"That's a good idee, Henry. I'll unbutton th' latch an' fluff up th' pillars fer 'im."

When she did not return, Henry led Jay to the bedroom where Martha still fussed about, lighting the lamps and making everything "just right" for the guest. "I propped open all th' winders wide," she said. "It'll be breezy in here afore long. If'n it gits too breezy, you can put 'em down."

"This was my niece Effie's room," Henry explained conversationally. "Joseph bought most o' th' furnishin's fer her, though some o' th' stuff b'longed to 'er own mother. She was born a cripple, an' Joseph favored 'er."

"What . . . what did you say her *name* was, Mr. Harris?" Henry interpreted the stricken look on Jay's face to be foot pain.

"Her name was Effie Harris, the only child o' my deceased brother, Charles Harris. Effie was born in th' Territory o' New Mexico right on th' claim where Joseph now ranches. Her mother departed this life when th' child was scarce three year old. An' me bein' Charles's only livin' relative an' all, he brung 'er here for us'ns to care fer while he took 'isself off to Californy to th' gold run. He planned to strike it rich an' return fer th' lassie, but he was amongst th' many unfortunate what lost their life in th' melee."

"And you . . . reared Effie?"

"We did our dead-level best, her bein' a cripple an' all. 'Twarn't always easy." Henry shifted uneasily at the memory.

Martha lowered her head. "I warn't much understandin' o' 'er crippled-up condition fer th' first few years."

"But after she saved our S—uh, one o' th' other childern from a fire, we all treated 'er real special, realizin' we'd be shorted a girl if'n hit hadn't been fer little Effie riskin' 'er life to rescue 'er," Henry continued.

"An' too, she's why we have this here nice place to live. We lived in a ragged ole shack o' a place, 'bout to cave in on us, an' that mortgaged to more'n its value on account o' a turrible drought. Then Effie was found out to be heir with half inter'st in 'er maternal grandparents' big estate back east in Kentucky. She paid off our mortgage an' built us this new dwellin' b'sides, out'n 'er big heart. Warn't never a more generous-hearted human bein' than what she was."

"Joseph called 'er our 'bent-winged angel,'" Martha supplied. "He explained it like it takes mighty brave little souls to live on this earth all bent up an' fightin' fer their lives—an' those kind o'childern come 'specially to earth to bring sunshine to us. She was shore an angel awright. Never was a sweeter creature God sent into this world, so helpless an' innocent . . ."

"We got th' scare o' our life th' day after 'er sixteenth birthday, though. We come in this here very room what was her sleeping room an' found 'er *gone*."

A sort of groan came from Jay, his face averted.

"Someone kidnapped 'er right out th' winder an' left a ransom note demandin' money if'n we ever wanted to see 'er alive ag'in." Martha and Henry tossed the story back and forth, each painting a stroke or two to complete the picture.

"Henry went in to town to fetch th' money—an' whiles he was gone, th' younger o' our boys found our Effie all gagged an' tied up in th' ole Robbins barn 'bout a mile from here where they'd run to git out o' a bad rainstorm. We figgered 'twas jest th' good Lord what directed them to take refuge in th' old shed . . ."

"I'm . . . sure it was," Jay spoke in a gravelly voice,

weighted with emotion.

"Th' boys brought 'er back home all asoak."

"They was two boys what did th' crime. One was a used-to-be neighbor o' our'n what lived on th' Robbins place fer 'bout half a year onct. Name o' Claude Grimes. His paw was a bootlegger. Th' other'n we never knowed who was. Claude got justice due 'im on a crime later on an' has been penned up somewhere fer several year now. I guess they never caught th' other'n, an' he's prob'ly still at large an' bad-hearted. I always hoped I never met up with 'im to know 'im . . ."

"I b'lieve Henry'd turn 'im in to th' law yet!"

"I wouldn't hesitate a minute."

"Th' barn burnt down jest a few hours after th' younguns got Effie out an' safe home. Someone from up above was shore watchin' out fer our bent-winged angel."

"You said earlier this evening, Mr. Harris, that your niece . . . died? Was that . . . Effie?" Jay kept his tortured eyes on his feet.

"She passed away like her mother an' father before her."

"How . . . old was she when she died?"

"Jest sixteen."

"Did she die of . . . pneumonia?"

"We don't rightly know what took 'er. She'd been injured in a fall an' . . ."

The room reeled before Jay, and he caught at the door facing for support.

"I think, Martha, that we need to let Jay lay down an' not burden 'im with th' details o' life's hardships that befell our lot," Henry concluded, noting Jay's ashen features. "He has enough troubles o' 'is own, an' he looks sick an' in need o' beddin' down." They stepped quickly from the room, leaving Jay to face his conscience alone.

"I'm so glad you fetched Jay home with you, Henry," admitted Martha in the privacy of their own room. "He seems most nigh like one o' my very own. Jest think, Henry, th' sorrowin' boy has nobody in th' whole world . . ."

"He's a'ready helped with th' great lonesome gap in my heart, Martha."

"Do you s'pose he'll stay on with us if'n we insist?"

"I shore hope so. He wants to go to college. He'd started out acrost country lookin' fer a town where he could work an' school at th' same time, an' I told 'im 'bout Th' Springs what has th' railroad shops an' a fine school, b'sides."

"I'd as lief send 'im to th' academy as one of my own, Henry. Mayhap we could jest adopt him. Then he'd be Spurgeon Jay Harris. I like that fer a name."

"He's too old to adopt, 'cept *heart* adoptin', Martha. Th' law don't change people's names after a certain age. I think 'tis eighteen."

"I wish . . ." Martha chopped off her sentence.

"What you wishin', Martha?"

"I was jest wishin' our restless girl would'a stayed home another day more. She could'a shore helped us in ennertainin' th' young man . . ."

"I was thinkin' on th' same thing."

"When I git some meat on 'is bones, Henry, he'll be awful handsome."

"That's what I'm afeared, Martha. An' all th' lasses in th' country'll be wantin' to come visit us!"

"Did you notice, Henry, that th' story o' our Effie bothered Jay somethin' fierce?" Martha asked her husband. "Wonder why?"

"Death is his fresh enemy, Martha."

"We hadn't ort to've talked it in 'is presence."

"Hindsight's better'n foresight."

"He was so anxious to know did she die o' *pneumonia . . .*"

"I kinda 'spected his grandma died o' pneumonia, though he never did say 'zactly. Th' word layed open a unhealed wound."

"He shore must'a loved 'er."

"He did. When first he mentioned 'er memory to me out in th' pasture, he called 'er his 'beloved' grandmother."

"That shows 'is insides."

"He has a tender middle."

"We'll take keerful care not to mention pneumonia . . . er Effie . . . no more."

"That'd be best."

"Do you think, Henry, if'n we take special care o' Jay, who has no earthly fam'ly to 'is name, that mayhap th' good Lord will in exchange, take care o' our youngest wherever she is t'night?"

"I think it'd shore work that way, Martha, under th' reapin' an' sowin' part o' th' Bible. Mayhap God sent Jay to us."

"Oh, I'm right shore He did, Henry." Martha, having not slept since Sally's departure, presently fell to snoring heavily. And Henry, his heart still sore and bleeding, whispered a prayer for his wayward daughter and then joined Martha in dreamless slumber.

But Jay closed the door and sank to his knees in anguish in the familiar room, his gaze fixed on the south window. *She had died . . . Effie had died!*

Chapter Six

Confession

*T*he gong of the grandfather clock hammered out the hour, its metered twang falling silent after discharging its four o'clock duty.

Jay lay staring into the black night, unable to shed the shackles of his past. Sleep had abandoned him, but memory had not.

As if cued by the clock, he climbed out the south window—the same window he had entered more than a decade ago. Little had changed to alter the site of the misdeed. The timeless live oak stood as a silent, adamant witness to the new seedlings that had missed the mischief.

A sharp snap of his fingers brought Patches bounding from his repose beneath the porch. The dog required no explanation, needed no warrant.

Jay knew the way to the Robbins place; the route was tattooed in his mind like a brand. There had been three of them the last time his feet covered this trail: himself, Claude Grimes, and Effie Harris.

Not a word unsealed Jay's lips until he reached his destination a mile away. Beside the charred ruins of the old structure, over which many seasons had passed, he dropped heavily to the ground, cradling his head in trembling hands. Then the torrent of remorse released itself on the patient animal.

"I tried to forget the whole ugly episode. But the winds of fate . . . they will not let me forget. Now I must live with my sin ever before my eyes. She's dead, Patches. Effie is dead. Did you hear me? And I helped kill her! How can I live with myself?" He reached for the comfort of the creature beside him. "When we camped on that river a few hours ago, I had no idea I had returned to the scene of my crime—the unforgettable, unforgiveable wrong that I did."

Jay's chest heaved with the burden he bore.

"Grandmother never learned about my sin, thank God. It would have killed her very soul. Then I would have been guilty of yet another death. A sin is far reaching, boy. Grandma used to say, 'If you don't get the button in the first loop right, all the others will be out of line.' I buttoned up the wrong loop when I got mixed up with Claude Grimes.

"Grandma didn't like for me to hang around with Claude. But he was big and tough—twice my size and seven years my senior—and . . . my idol. Having no father, I sorely needed a role model. I tried to walk and talk like Claude Grimes.

"The more Grandmother denounced him, the more I defended him. Even the nickname he gave me—Spurs—

galled her. 'I gave you a good Christian name, and this young man is attempting to desecrate it,' she declared.

"One day Claude told me that he needed my help in a little job 'down south' where he used to live and that we would both make some big money. A 'cake job' he called it. It boosted my ego to think he chose me to help him.

"I'd been helping a neighbor man lay crossties for the railroad, and I told Grandma that my job was sending me out of town for a few days.

"She didn't want me to leave her, and of course, I knew deep down that I shouldn't go along with Claude. But we were all the way here before he told me what the job was. He planned an out-and-out kidnapping."

The dog had not moved. "Are you asleep, Patches?"

The dog's tail beat a staccato on the leaf-strewn turf.

"I tried to act brave, but inside I wanted to get out of it all and go home. I wished a thousand times I hadn't come. When I weakened, Claude held me with threats. His outbursts of insane rage when anything crossed him terrified me. I was too young to realize the effects of the bottle he had with him.

"We came here. This had once been Claude's home, and he knew his way around. After dark, we slipped over to the Harris house to get the lay of the land. The whole community congregated there to celebrate Effie's birthday, giving us an added advantage. We located her room, stole the bucket of homemade ice cream that Mr. Harris had set just outside the back door, and crept back to the old shed to wait.

"Claude passed his bottle to me, and the grog I drank burned my throat like acid. 'I brought you along to write

49

the ransom note,' he said. 'I went to school with those Harris children, and if I write it myself, they might recognize my handwriting.' Would God that had been the extent of my involvement!

"He instructed me to demand a thousand dollars, which, he said, we'd split between us. He knew about Effie's inheritance and he knew the Harris family would give any amount for her life.

"The more Claude drank, the meaner he got. This was a side of Claude that I had never seen, and it frightened me.

"We went back in the darkest part of the night—just before dawn—crawled in the south window, and scared the girl so badly that she passed out. It pleased Claude that she lost consciousness, but I almost cried when I saw how small and crippled-up she was. I remember asking myself what if she was my little sister.

"We brought her here, bound and gagged her, and laid her on the damp, cold floor."

The black velvet of night wore thin. A nesting mockingbird, awakened by Jay's confessional, impatiently began her call for dawn. Jay looked up, saw nothing but the tree's shape, and continued his monologue.

"When the girl regained her senses, she amazed me. I knew that she must be scared, but she never once cried out. In fact, there was a . . . peace about her that unnerved me.

"About midmorning, I got hungry. Claude knew where a cellar was that had canned goods stored in it. While we were gone, a gully-washer of a storm came up, and we stayed holed up in the cellar until the rain let up. It was while we were in that cellar that the younger Harris boys took refuge in the barn and found Effie."

The first rays of sun burned off the predawn fog, bringing into focus the perimetrical remains of the razed building. Jay arose and paced the premises, unheeding of the pain in his foot. The ache in his heart superseded any other pang.

"We came back and found Effie gone. I knew in my heart that a Higher Power had taken Effie's case, and I begged Claude to abandon the project and take me home. But he was determined to waylay Mr. Harris on his way home from the bank and have the ransom money. A chill, born of fear, set me to shaking, and I begged Claude to build me a fire. I fell asleep and awakened to Claude's violent temper, as he demanded me to wake up and go with him.

"We hid in the bushes beside the road—that road you and I just crossed. When we heard the horse coming, Claude demanded that I step out into the road and stop the horse and rider."

Closing his eyes, Jay relived the bitter scene. "It wasn't Mr. Harris on the horse; it was the sheriff. He shot, and the bullet scarcely missed my head as Claude dragged me back into the protection of the brush and we scrambled for cover. We ran for our lives.

"It's certainly not a pleasant memory, Patches."

The young man picked his way through the shed's skeletal remains, stumbling over the lid of the old iron stove. "Here's what's left of the old stove that set the place afire. I'm glad she wasn't burned to death.

"Mrs. Harris said she was injured in a fall. I suppose she must have tried to get up with her hands tied and fell and hurt herself. But . . . I feel sure she died of exposure.

51

She was so frail, it looked like it wouldn't take much to finish her off. I told Claude I was afraid she'd take pneumonia, but he scoffed and said it would take a few days for her to die of it and by then we would have our money and be gone.

"So, you see, Patches, I'm a murderer. Did you hear what I said? A *murderer*. Mr. and Mrs. Harris have no idea that I'm the one who helped Claude Grimes commit the murder. I'm as much to blame as Claude because I wrote the note. Mr. Harris said last evening that if he ever found out who the guilty man was, he would turn him over to the law yet."

Jay sighed, a sound that burst forth from the roots of his soul. "Claude got his dues, but what's to become of me?"

The sore distress in the voice of his master brought a plaintive whine from Patches.

"Now I've got to make some decisions, boy. The easy thing to do would be to run from myself and try to forget again. But that's the coward's way. Grandmother wouldn't consider that honorable. And neither would God."

Man and dog sat immobile, while two forces in Jay's soul struggled for supremacy. The woods stirred with life; a hawk dipped and screamed as he sought prey for his breakfast. The foliage, colorless by night, took on a tint of deep green. Scattered here and there in variegated patches, stood the beautiful buttercups on their delicate stems, while clumps of larkspur swelled with bloom and leaf buds.

At length, Jay arose, squared his shoulders, and lifted his chin resolutely. Patches stood at attention.

"What I must do is stay right here and find a way to make up to this family for the years of grief I have caused them. I'll gladly give them my life for hers, though mine is not nearly as valuable. I should have made restitution long ago, but I had Grandmother to care for until now. And besides, I didn't know that . . . Effie died.

"I don't know how one could repay such an indebtedness. But the day will come when my chance will come to repay my debt! I'll pray and ask God to grant it. And I'll know when my opportunity comes—and I won't hesitate to fulfill my obligation to the Harris family, in life or in death. Then I can go . . . honorably.

"I know that God forgave me when He saved me. But I can't forgive myself until I have made the proper restitution.

"I guess God sent us here for a reason, Patches. I don't believe in mere happenstances. Not when one is a Christian. Come on, boy. Let's go back to the house and do whatever we can to make up for lost time."

Chapter Seven

Shocking Reality

"*M*ay I have a cup of water, please?" Sally awoke from her troubled sleep to find Mrs. Gordon bending over her anxiously. The blinding sun fell aslant across the room, striking her eyes harshly. Her head throbbed mercilessly, and her cheeks felt afire. Terrible cramps gripped her about the middle. Pauper's burial . . . unmarked grave . . . the heinous words still echoed.

"Oh, you're finally awake! I thought I'd have to call the county mortician for sure," Mrs. Gordon declared soberly, adding to Sally's discomfort. "Wouldn't have known who else to call."

"Water . . ." repeated Sally, weakly.

"Room service is two bits a day, Miss," Mrs. Gordon hid her vulnerable nature under a calloused bark. "Special services take extra time, and we're running short-handed already. If I catered to all fifteen tenants, I wouldn't get anything else done. And if I start catering free, I'll have everybody playing sick all time just to get food brought to their rooms."

Sally pointed toward her handbag. At that moment, she would have given her entire purse for a drink of cool water.

Mrs. Gordon padded leadenly back with the water, and Sally gulped it down eagerly. It tasted lukewarm and brackish. Then another violent cramp seized her, and she doubled with a groan.

"There's a nurse that boards here, Harriet. Her name is Miss Banks. When she finishes her shift, I'll send her up to prescribe a tonic if you'd like. She probably wouldn't charge much."

"Please send her," Sally whispered, her eyes bright with pain.

All day Sally tossed on the stony bed, snatches of forgotten prayers stealing from her parched lips, her life passing before her in a sketchy panorama. The "freedom" she once dreamed of had turned out quite differently from the enticing picture her fancy had painted.

She yearned for the Brazos Point farm and the touch of her mother's hand. But the mortal in her, still able to speak, reminded her that the farm had become but a dead sea with no outlet. The last lonely year she had spent there loomed in her memory like a graveyard for her youthful spirit. She reminded her pricking conscience that she had not had an escort to a social function since her graduation more than a year ago. And there seemed little hope of any in the future.

Molly Rushing, the church organist's controversial granddaughter and Sally's only close "friend" had taken herself to The Springs and signed on as a soda jerk to relieve her boredom. Since then, Sally had watched her character deteriorate to what Martha termed a "flapper." She painted her face, went to picture shows with young men she hardly knew, and flirted shamelessly, "laying her name on people's tongues," as Martha would say. Her unbecoming behavior worked adversely for Sally; Martha equated Molly's dissipation with all public employment. The only occupation the old-fashioned mother considered decent for a young lady was teaching school as Amy and Dessie had done. And Sally could not picture herself a schoolmarm, imprisoned in school walls.

Her thoughts, aided by the fever, jumped about like an unpredictable cricket to Brazos Point and back again and then settled on the interim boat ride. Her body still felt the rhythmical sway of the river's ebb and flow.

She recalled the strange sensation of her first day afloat. *It was while I hovered near the shore to benefit from the cooling shadows of the arching trees that I felt as though someone was watching me. Oddly though, the impression did not make me uncomfortable. No, it was as if that someone stood near to protect me.*

Sally's mind reconstructed the railroad trestle standing ahead of her like a great spined creature with wooden legs, supported by giant square feet wading in the water. She remembered looking about and feeling the need to straighten her hair to be presentable to this unseen friend.

No houses were in evidence, but a dog appeared in a small clearing for a brief moment. *Or did I imagine the dog? No, I remember distinctly what he looked like—short ears and many colors like a patchwork quilt! The dog was no figment of my imagination.*

Since there was a dog, there must have been someone nearby.

In and out of sleep Sally journeyed, eating none of the greasy soup Mrs. Gordon sent to her, unable to focus her mind for long on any course of action for the days that loomed ahead, and weary with the effort of trying. Reason and incoherence tangled so that she could not think clearly. Sometimes she thought she saw her mother's face between her and the decrepit doorway of the room.

The nurse, a sweet, sad-eyed woman of indeterminate age, found Sally crying.

"My little lamb," she crooned gently. "Don't you cry. We'll have you up and going again just in time."

"In time for what?" Sally murmured.

"Why, in time for whatever it was you came here for."

"I . . . don't know why I came here," sobbed Sally.

The nurse, accustomed to the emotional valleys of her patients, pulled up the frayed cane-bottom chair and stationed herself beside the distraught girl, patting her feverish arm.

"Then perhaps we can discuss it and try to decide." Her tired smile seemed to take great effort. "Let's start at the beginning by telling me who you are and where you are from."

"I'm Sal . . . Harriet. And I live . . . used to live on a farm."

"Mrs. Gordon tells me you now have no family."

A tear squeezed from Sally's closed eyes, but she made no reply.

"Life is bleak without dear ones, isn't it? The most

precious gift God gave to any girl in the world is a mother. He put flowers in bunches and stars in galaxies, but mothers were so special, He just made one apiece. Why, just today I stood by the bedside of a dying mother and made a feeble effort to comfort her weeping daughter, about your same age I'd guess."

Sally turned her head away.

"How old are you, Harriet?"

"Eighteen."

"When did you leave home?" The question caught Sally offguard as Miss Banks hoped it would.

"I . . ."

"Harriet, if I am to help you, you must be truthful with me."

"You won't . . . tell?"

"You can trust me not to tell. Unless my better judgment dictates that I should."

"I left home Saturday morning."

"By train?"

"No, ma'am. I floated down the Brazos River in my brother's small boat."

"How long were you exposed to the insects and heat?"

"A part of three days and two nights."

"Did you eat anything?"

"Yes ma'am. I had several pieces of chicken my moth . . . I packed for the trip."

"What else, Harriet? This is important."

"A sweet potato, a tin of beans, some biscuits, and some cake."

"Did you eat out of the tin more than one day?"

"Just a few bites. The beans tasted funny."

"Have you had any stomach cramps?"

"Yes."

"You probably have a touch of food poisoning, Harriet. Your food probably got too warm and started to spoil. The leftover tin of food or the chicken—or the combination of both—made you ill. I think you'll be all right. We'll give you a good purgative and then some warm milk."

"How long will it take?"

"To get the medicine and milk?"

"No, for me to get well."

"You'll likely be weak for two or three days yet."

"As soon as I am able to travel, Miss Banks, I'll board the westbound train and go back home."

"That's the wisest thing you could possibly do, Harriet."

"My name is really Sally Harris."

"Good luck, Sally." Nurse Banks patted her arm, a real smile now replacing the forced one. "Give your mother a big hug for me." Her eyes were moist.

Just before dark, the nurse brought the medicine, the milk, and a small basket of fresh fruit. She straightened Sally's coverlet, fluffed her humpy pillow, then bent to kiss her good night.

The kiss comforted Sally's racked heart, and before she fell asleep, she offered a prayer of thanksgiving for Miss Banks, a friend in this "far country." She would be a confidante, a sympathetic listener, kind and caring. God surely sent her!

But Sally saw Miss Banks no more. Mrs. Gordon said she was called away on a "live-in" case and had checked out of the boarding house hurriedly. Sally felt a great loss, accompanied by black depression.

With the inferior food and stuffy room, strength crept back slowly. And when at last her illness had spent itself, so had her scant funds. With a sinking heart, she found that she hadn't enough left for a train ticket home! The terrible realization scorched its way into her soul.

Chapter Eight

The Parson's Visit

*B*efore the week was out, Pastor Stevens called at the Harris residence to learn the reason for Martha and Henry's absence from church the Sunday past. His initial surprise was the unfamiliar multicolored dog that met him at the front porch.

His next surprise was finding that neither Martha nor Henry was ill. "We was jest good-Samaritanin', Pastor," Martha told him, glad that she did not have to confess her all-night cry over Sally. "Henry found a young man all down an' out camped b'side th' river on our property an' brung him here fer me to fix fer—a Sunday at that! Husbands er mighty unpredictable. But th' boy he brung is a likeable chap, an' right helpful, too. He's out back helpin' Henry with th' feedin' now."

"You weren't afraid, Sister Harris, to take in a complete stranger with a girl the age of Sally in the household?"

Martha cleared her throat. "No, I warn't afeared. An' in anywise, th' poor man couldn't go on no further. He had wretched blisters on 'is feet what had got theirselves infected, an' he couldn't hardly walk. You know what th' Bible says 'bout takin' in folks; some has took in angels an' didn't know it."

"Does he plan to stay on awhile, Sister Harris?"

"Why, I shore hope he does!"

Pastor Stevens gave her a puzzled frown. "Then I guess he'll be coming along with you and Brother Harris and Sally to church?"

"I 'spect so."

"Good. We need a growth in the younger section of the church."

"We needed that a long time 'fore now."

"What we need is some move-ins instead of so many move-outs."

"We ain't got much fer to attract young folks."

"Young folks ought not have to have special programs to attach them to the church. I say all such gimmicks as socials and ice cream parties and games are carnal and lead the church to worldliness."

Martha opened her mouth to speak, probably out of turn, but fortunately Henry and Jay came in the back door, chatting companionably. "Oh, here comes Henry an' our guest now, Brother Stevens. I'm right anxious that you meet Jay."

Henry introduced Jay to the pastor, and Brother Stevens accepted Henry's invitation to take a chair and acquaint himself with Jay Walls.

"Have you ever been in these parts before?" asked the parson by way of friendly conversation.

Jay stammered, too honest to lie, yet unprepared for the premature revelation of his past.

"Of course he hain't, pastor," Martha spoke up mercifully. "He's from up northwest o' this state, most nigh to th' edge o' Oklahoma. We're doin' our best to acquaint 'im with our area, though."

The pastor nodded, satisfied.

"Care fer some tea, Pastor?"

Brother Stevens nodded, and Martha disappeared into the kitchen.

"Can you fetch me some fresh, cool water from th' well, Henry?" she called to her husband, and he hastened away to her assistance.

"Are you a Christian, Mr. Walls?" The pastor had a habit of getting to the point without detours.

"Yes, sir."

"What church membership are you?"

"I've not attended regular church services for several years, sir. I read my Bible and rely upon God to guide me."

"Choosing one's own Scriptures is both unwise and unsafe," expostulated the preacher. "One needs a parent church."

"I . . . hadn't the privilege of church attendance since I was obliged to care for my invalid grandmother. I would have been glad to avail myself of the opportunity had it been offered me. And what you say about choosing one's own Scriptures is true if one goes to the Word to substantiate his or her own theory or to find justification for what one wishes to believe; it can result in serious consequences. However, sir, such was not the case with me. My heart was open and honest."

"Then, of course, you do embrace the doctrines of our church fathers?"

65

"It depends upon what that doctrine is, sir, and if it corresponds with the Bible."

"The blessed trinity . . ."

"What is that, sir?"

"God in three persons: God the Father is one person; Jesus, the Son, is the second person; the Holy Ghost is the third person."

"Three people?"

"Yes. All hold equal power to be sure."

"I . . . is that in the Bible, sir?"

"Most certainly."

"I'm sorry, but I have studied the Bible thoroughly, and I haven't found any such doctrine."

"I fear you are in gross error."

"I did not find the Holy Ghost to be a person, but a Spirit. Jesus said, 'A spirit hath not flesh and bones.' Sir, when Jesus went away, He promised to send 'the Comforter, which is the Holy Ghost.' On the Day of Pentecost, the Holy Ghost fell upon those who tarried in the upper room in Jerusalem. Surely you will agree that it was not a *person* who fell?"

Brother Stevens reddened, frustrated and annoyed. "Where are you quoting from?"

"Luke 24:39 and John 14:26."

"Your memory is amazing."

"I spent many days with the Bible, sir. Grandmother loved for me to read aloud to her."

"Then, according to your Bible study, there are only two persons in the Godhead?"

"No, sir. God is a Spirit. He's everywhere."

"Now, you don't mean . . ."

"Do you have a Bible, Pastor? John tells us that God

is a Spirit in chapter four, verse twenty-four."

"Mr. Walls, God was the Father of our Lord Jesus Christ. Everyone knows that!"

"Well, sir, the Bible also says that Mary was found with child of the Holy Ghost. It would seem that God and the Holy Ghost are one and the same, would it not? My references are Matthew 1:18 and Luke 1:35."

"Well . . ."

"That leaves Jesus as the only *person* of the Godhead—that's why He is called the 'only begotten Son.' And 'in him dwelleth all the fulness of the Godhead bodily' according to Colossians 2:9. Paul also wrote that God was in Christ, reconciling the world unto Himself."

"Mr. Walls, you will find that we hold strictly to tradition."

"The tradition of the Bible or of a denomination?"

"We are nondenominational."

"Then how do you baptize, Pastor?"

"By immersion, using the words Father, Son and Holy Ghost."

"I beg your pardon, sir, but in my search for truth, I read everything I could get my hands on about the original church that Christ started in the Book of Acts. Fortunately, I had access to a good library in our city. I found that church leaders gradually changed the mode of baptism from the name of Jesus to the formula you mention. Originally, every Christian was baptized in the name of Jesus as instructed in Acts 2:38. Jesus Himself said in Matthew, 'Go ye therefore, and teach all nations, baptizing them in the *name* of . . .' "

"That's the Scripture! That's the one we use—'in the name of the Father, and of the Son, and of the Holy Ghost!' "

67

"Yes, pastor, but you are not fulfilling that Scripture. It says to baptize in the *name,* and Father is not the name. Neither is Son or Holy Ghost. The only name given among men whereby we must be saved is the name of Jesus."

Wishing to change the tenor of the discourse, the pastor asked abruptly, "How long have you been saved, Mr. Walls?"

"I received the Acts two experience when I was seventeen. And I sorely needed salvation. I had a pretty black record, I'm afraid."

"The Acts two experience?"

"Yes, sir. God added me to His church just like He did the first converts. I received the Holy Ghost and spoke with tongues as the Spirit gave utterance."

"That's not for us today."

" 'For the promise is unto you, and to your children, and to all that are afar off . . .' " quoted Jay, his face aglow.

"I'll have to say one thing for you, Mr. Walls. You are sincere in what you believe." Pastor Stevens again tried to circumvent the subject. "You will join Brother and Sister Harris and Sally for service with us the Sunday next, will you not? I'm sure Sally will be glad to have someone younger . . ."

Jay looked bewildered. "Who is Sally?"

"Sally Harris. Brother and Sister Harris's youngest daughter. You haven't met her?"

"No, sir. I have not had the pleasure of meeting Sally."

Now the pastor looked bewildered. "Well, I wonder where Sally . . ."

Martha entered with the tea, making profuse apologies for the lengthy delay. "Henry had some trouble at th' well, Brother Stevens. He had no plans o' jest desertin' you. Th' rope broke an' he had to fix it afore I could get some fresh water."

"That's quite all right, Sister Harris. Mr. Walls and I were having a . . . uh, discussion on the Bible."

"Did you know, Pastor, that Henry is havin' us one o' them talkin' boxes put in? We made th' decision last night."

"You're speaking of a telephone?"

"Yes, sir. Henry avowed when they was first invented that he'd have one o'er his dead body. He hated 'um, callin' 'um women's gossip boxes." Martha gave a victor's chuckle. "But he changed his mind. We thought we'd best git one so's if'n any word came from Sal . . ."

She blushed for having forgotten that the parson knew nothing of Sally's departure.

Chapter Nine

Sally's Decision

"When you're through lading the table, Harriet, there's a man in the southwest guestroom that wants a plate lunch brought to his room. He's an important businessman, so be careful to choose the best cut of meat and the whitest napkin for his tray."

Mrs. Gordon gave the crisp order to Sally as she hurried back and forth from the kitchen stove to the long dining table, her flushed cheeks suggesting overwork. Mrs. Gordon added a new duty with each new sunrise, until it seemed to Sally that one more task stacked atop the pyramid would surely topple the whole of her constitution. She had cooked most of the meal today; Mrs. Gordon had gotten sidetracked.

This had, in fact, been the busiest day in all the nightmare of time since Mrs. Gordon hired her. Could that have been a mere two weeks ago? Her mind reenacted

71

the morning that the landlady found her weeping, her packed travel case beside her.

"What's wrong, Harriet?"

Sally could not tell if the controlled voice masked sympathy or derision.

"I find that I . . . haven't enough money left for a ticket back . . . to where I came from . . . or to stay on here another week . . ."

"What had you planned to do, Harriet, before you fell ill?"

"Get a job."

Mrs. Gordon's scrutinizing look made Sally drop her eyes.

"I haven't the money to lend you for a ticket. I have the food bill and mortgage to pay this week. If I lent money to every indigent that crossed my threshold, I'd have been bankrupt long since."

"I'm not seeking your benevolence, ma'am." Thinking back now, Sally remembered drawing her shoulders up proudly.

Mrs. Gordon apparently ignored her. "But I am dreadfully in need of kitchen help. I cannot give you any money, of course, but I'll provide you your room and board and small personal needs in exchange for your help. You'll be obliged to arise before daylight to help with breakfast and retire only after the last skillet has been scoured at night, you understand."

The offer had seemed a godsend, a solution to her hopeless dilemma. Sally had meekly followed Mrs. Gordon to the scullery, donned a cheap, muslin apron and begun her new job.

Now she felt trapped in a more hopeless cycle with

no prospects of escape. If hearts could drown, Sally felt hers would. For instead of the flood of tears spilling down her hot cheeks as they begged to do, she held them in reserve until they formed a backwash in her heart.

Sometimes Sally entertained the woeful thought that a demon had laid claim to her soul in the form of this fleshy proprietress. The woman had demanded the last two bits from Sally's purse, leaving not even a penny for postage to write home and ask her father to come for her. The demand came when Mrs. Gordon found Sally with her light burning late one night.

"I can't pay the gas bill for you to sit up and fritter away the time you should be sleeping," she snarled, asking for the change the girl had left to help defray the added expense. Did she suspect that Sally sat up composing a letter that, if mailed, would bring her release?

An avalanche of bitter tears, pouring onto the letter, dimmed the words she had written but did nothing to erase the despair engraved in her heart. She had eventually shred the letter into bits and tossed it into the stove lest unkind eyes read it.

"You're spilling the gravy, Harriet!" Mrs. Gordon hauled Sally back to the present with a jolt, her imperious inflection of the strange name causing Sally to despise the alias she had chosen for herself. "Give more attention to what you are doing!"

"Yes, ma'am."

Boarders gathered, preoccupied and expecting the same tasteless food. But Sally, reared on the farm and trained by a farm mother accustomed to cooking for harvest hands, was a good cook.

The whispers, curiosity, and open compliments over

the well-prepared food may have lifted Sally's flagging spirits had she heard them. However, Mrs. Gordon's urgent command with regard to the southwest room's guest took her away from the boarders' comments to another of her ceaseless duties.

Her rebellious little curls played havoc about her pretty face, their habit when aided by perspiration, as she hurried to take the teatowel covered tray to the quarters Mrs. Gordon indicated.

She hesitated at the open door, left ajar by the occupant for the benefit of any chance breeze. When the gentleman did not look up, she entered and set about to arrange his food on the small oak table. This room, larger and better furnished than the others, obviously housed only special guests.

The man worked at a roll-top desk near the window, plans and papers scattered about. His just graying hair swooped into a wave from one deep cowlick on the right side of his forehead, making him the handsomer.

Wordlessly, Sally arranged the table, the silver, the napkin, and the water pitcher. Then she said shyly, "Sir, your lunch is ready."

When he looked up to acknowledge her announcement, the intense blue of his gentle eyes caught her by surprise. "Thank you, little lady."

"Is there anything else I can do for you, sir?"

"It all looks heavenly." He smiled then, his eyes sweeping across the plate. "You're new here, aren't you?"

"I've been working here for two weeks."

"Perhaps we should get acquainted. I room here frequently. I'm Seth Cotterby with the Telephone Company."

"I'm Sal . . . Harriet."

"I'm pleased to meet you, Miss Harriet. And I see by the food that Mrs. Gordon has apparently hired in a new cook, too, has she not?"

"I don't believe so, sir."

"Hmmm . . . she's surely improved on her cooking since last I stayed here. This is the cleanest lodge in town, but the food was sorely lacking in eye appeal—until now."

Sally dismissed herself and fled back to the dining room lest Mrs. Gordon accuse her of dallying; she found a certain refuge from her boss amid the clatter of dishes.

"Did you pick up Mr. Cotterby's china?" Mrs. Gordon asked when the dining room had been cleared.

"I . . . forgot." Sally dried her hands on a treadbare towel and darted away before Mrs. Gordon could scold.

Mr. Cotterby's room was empty, but on the tray lay a shiny dime with a note that read, "A tip for my efficient waitress." Sally snatched it up eagerly, joyously. *A stamp! I can buy a stamp! Mr. Cotterby's ten cents will liberate me from this dungeon!*

Sally tried to maintain a steady, controlled countenance to hide the exultant thrill in her breast precipitated by the dime hidden in her apron pocket. She had almost reached the swinging doors leading into the scullery when Mrs. Gordon called her back, accosting her in a grating voice. "Did Mr. Cotterby leave a tip? He generally does."

"Yes, ma'am. He left me a dime."

"*You* a dime? Young lady, the dime is not yours! To take it would be flagrant dishonesty on your part. I never allow my maids to keep tips. That dime goes to defray the expenses of this boarding house. With prices like they are now, it takes every penny to stave off a foreclosure. And if that should happen, neither you nor I will have a bed to sleep on. You came here a homeless waif, so you should value this lodging." If her intentions were to make Sally feel like a thief, she succeeded.

That dark evening, Sally searched her soul and found an empty cupboard with no inner resources left; she could endure no more. She lay awake, trembling under the day's injustices. The night deepened, erasing clusters of stars here and there as the patchwork of clouds thickened.

At length she got up and dressed in her best dress. She packed her gripsack lightly, too tired to manage a heavy burden. Most of her clothing would be left behind; Martha would replenish her wardrobe once she got home.

When the house quieted, its dwellers all asleep, Sally let herself silently out the front door and headed for the river. Once convinced that rowing upstream would be a hopeless impossibility, her desperate mind refused to admit that any means of escape was an impossibility now. Food? She even reasoned away the need for food, telling herself that she would search out berries, nuts, and wild apples along the shoreline to sustain herself on her journey home.

She kept to the shadows, bypassing the dens of iniquity. Confusing night noises arose from somewhere, but in her rapid flight, she took no time to analyze them. Her single goal was to reach the boat landing where her boat was docked and be on her way home, away from this detestable place forever.

Near the river, dew glistened on the grass as the fitful moon hopscotched in and out of the patchy clouds, now and then shedding an unexpected brightness. A giddiness

76

took hold of her as she neared the place where, less than three weeks ago, she had tied the boat built by her brother's own hands.

She made her way among the brush to the short rocky beach, remembering every detail of the path she had taken. Ah, there was the tree that anchored her craft!

She stopped, puzzled, sure that this was the place she had left it. Or was it? The boat was gone.

Wily Molly

*W*ord traveled fast.

Before long, Molly Rushing knew through Sister Myrt who found out from Sister Stevens who was informed by her husband that the Harris household housed a male guest, unmarried and "easy on th' eyes."

So Molly Rushing made immediate plans to spend the weekend with her doting grandmother in Brazos Point and see this new apparition for herself—even if she had to go to church to do so. No eligible man escaped her scrutiny.

Molly's eagerness to accompany her to church on the Lord's Day astonished and pleased her gullible grandmother. "I've been thinking lately, Granny Myrt, that I may be missing out on a good thing by not attending church on Lord's Day." Molly had mastered the art of deception long ago and knew all the chinks in her grandparent's armor.

But on Sunday morning when Molly appeared with a round of rouge on each cheek flaming pink below ice blue eyes, her hair marcelled and crimped, Myrt feebly tried to object. "Pastor Stevens ain't much for outward adornin', Molly. I shouldn't think you'd wish to provide him material for a sermon. You should be more modest for church services."

"Oh, pooh, Granny Myrt! We're living in modern days, not in the antediluvian age!" scorned Molly. "Brother Stevens has too many hidebound ideas and narrow views. That's exactly why he doesn't attract more young folks. By the way, how is Sally Harris getting on with the new gent at her house?"

"I ain't seen hide ner hair o' Sally Harris. She ain't been to church since th' young whippersnapper came. When I ask Martha 'bout her, she gets mumlike. Nobody can be more shut-mouthed than Marthy Harris when she's a mind to."

"Maybe Sally's gone away to Dessie's for the summer." Molly had a penchant for speaking her wishful thinking aloud.

"Mayhap she has."

Molly entered the church that Sunday with an air of patronizing God and took a seat behind the Harris pew, impatiently awaiting their arrival. She arranged and re-arranged her soft silk frock in becoming folds about her, touching the knot of coral ribbon in her raven-black hair to assure herself that it was still in place. Myrt took her place at the antiquated organ, with her perpetual "religious" frown.

Pastor Stevens shook Molly's hand; Myrt, watching sleuthfully, caught his displeased look. "Been a spell since you churched with us," he said, towering in the aisle. At that moment, Henry and Martha Harris—along with Jay—slipped into their pew, and Molly's attention joined them, leaving the pastor talking to the back of her head.

As the service struggled on, Molly's carnal mind connived ways and schemes to impress Jay. She wondered where Sally was and when she would be returning and where this young eligible man with the gorgeous head of hair hailed from. Pastor Stevens's sermon fell on deaf ears. Molly heard nothing of his warnings against "modern-day vices," probably directed toward her. It was not for the benefit of her soul that she had come to church this morning, and for dismissal she longed. Since she sat behind the attraction, he could not very well exit without seeing her.

"When will our Sister Sally be returning?" the parson asked Martha when church let out. "We're missing her."

Molly saw her lower her eyes self-consciously. "I'm . . . I'm not right shore, parson. She may be away . . . all summer. Then ag'in she may decide to come on home next week." Molly listened, a cunning smile surfacing on her face.

When Jay stepped out into the crowded aisle, so did Molly. She offered her gloved hand and smiled bewitchingly. "I'm Molly Rushing. We're just ever so pleased to have you worship with us. I work in The Springs and don't get to come *every* Sunday, but seeing someone handsomely young at our church is most refreshing."

Jay, unaccustomed to girls or their flattery, met her beguiling violet eyes with a glad, innocent smile of response. "My name is Jay Walls. The pleasure of meeting

81

is mine, I'm sure. I'm working for Mr. Harris just now, but after harvest, I'll be looking for another position elsewhere."

"Oh, you surely must come to The Springs! It's a growing city with many opportunities for work with fast advancement. They call it the young man's town."

They moved outside, still conversing. Martha watched Jay protectively out of the corner of her eye; Molly's silvery laugh grated on her nerves. It sounded practiced and artificial.

"Will you take lunch with Grandmother and me?" Martha heard and set her lips.

"Why, I would be delighted," Jay answered, falling like a captured thing into the trap. "I'll tell the Harrises . . ." A feeling of bitter resentment shot an arrow through Martha's heart. She wanted to step between Jay and the deadly danger but could only stand aside helplessly, eyeing Molly frostily.

"Grandmother, Mr. Walls has agreed to join us for lunch. Isn't that just too wonderful?" What pleased Molly pleased Myrt. She smiled at her progeny's coy manners.

"That no-'count granddaughter o' Myrt's is puttin' one over on our Jay," Martha burst out when she and Henry reached a safe, out-of-earshot zone. "He don't know nuthin' 'bout brassy girls. Did you see 'er flit 'er eyes an' shine up to 'im? I don't like it no little bit, Henry! I don't . . ."

"Now, Martha, Jay is of age . . ."

"But he ain't smart in th' ways o' wickedness. He's been shut away from society. I'm gonna warn 'im . . ."

"You ain't gonna do no sech thing, Martha. Who he has dinner with ain't none o' our business. We ain't 'is

boss. An' if'n you start tryin' to boss 'im like he was a
kid in knickers, he'll up an' leave us. You'll make big trouble fer us if'n you go runnin' down Myrt's granddaughter,
too. Myrt'll hear o' it an' crank up a big stink at church."

"I ain't willin' to sit idle by an' see as good a boy as
Jay Walls hornswoggled by a sody jerk what paints 'er
face an' crimps 'er hair."

"Best you talk to th' good Lord 'bout it than anyone
else."

"I wisht Sally was here. *She'd* tell 'im."

"Well, she ain't."

"I don't want to be reminded that she ain't."

"You brung it up."

"Do you think she'll ever come back, Henry?"

"All childern eventually come back, Martha."

"I'd'a thought she'd'a come back afore now."

"I would'a, too."

Meanwhile, Molly congratulated herself on the suc-
cess of her well-laid plan. Jay fell for her ploy easier than
she had expected. The hook was right; the bait was
right—now all she had to do was pull him in.

It must be said of Molly that she recognized quality
in men, though quality was by no means a requirement
for her admiration. Here was a man with character, his
firm chin showing a combination of strength, courage,
and nobility.

Molly's subtle flirtations pleased Jay. He had never
been in a position for girls to give him attention. The
delicious new experience made him heady. So ignorant
was he of the wiles of worldly women that the fakeness
of her piety escaped him entirely.

Myrt brought forth her best fine china, serving the

most lavish meal afforded by her food supply. She was proud of Molly's progress with this charming, self-controlled gentleman. Molly certainly needed a level-headed man to settle her down! Reports of her post-midnight dances and reveling had reached Myrt's ears.

"Why don't we take a walk in the woods and enjoy God's great creation?" Molly suggested after the meal, giving her grandmother a playful wink.

"A lovely idea!" Jay agreed, a pawn in her hand.

The sighing cedars and arching hackberry trees, richly plagued with boughs of mistletoe, added to the pleasure of the summer walk. Molly called attention to flowers "dressed in their Sunday best."

"Tell me all about yourself," she coaxed.

"There's not much to tell, I'm afraid." he laughed lightly. "No golden apples hang from my family tree."

"How old are you?"

"I'm just behind twenty-five."

"And still single?" her laughter rippled. "How did you manage that?"

"Well, I . . . haven't had the advantage of courting. Until a few weeks ago, I spent my leisure time caring for my invalid grandmother."

"How sad!" Molly widened her eyes becomingly.

"Oh, I didn't mind at all; I owed her a great deal, you see. She reared me . . . and sacrificed to send me to school."

"How . . . brave!" Molly quickly adapted her evaluation to Jay's mood. "But now you need to *live*."

"This . . . is living," hoping his words would please her.

Molly led him on. "Look!" She touched his arm. "Isn't

the honeysuckle blossom just splendid? I think that is my favorite plant!''

Enchanted by Molly's fragile loveliness, Jay plunged into the thicket, returning with a trellis of the honeysuckle whose intoxicating perfume filled the air about them. On a sudden impulse, he tucked a tiny spray of it in her dark hair.

"Oh, you're sweet!" she purred. "Thank you. I've never met anyone quite so *thoughtful.*"

"You're quite wonderful, yourself." Jay reddened, wondering at the words that flowed from his mouth so easily, yet unbidden.

"Do you plan to marry someday?"

"Why . . . I hadn't thought of it much. But, yes, I suppose I do . . . someday."

"Have you anyone in particular in mind . . . just yet?"

"No. I saw one girl I thought I could love . . . before today, that is . . ." Jay stopped, confused at his mixed emotions. "But I didn't even know her name and will probably never see her again."

"Did you meet her . . . here?" asked the wily Molly.

"No, she was boating several miles downriver."

Molly Rushing looked into Jay's handsome face and decided that her next move was worth the calculated risk. So she purposefully stumbled and in falling grabbed his arm for support. Alarmed, he gently sat her back on her feet.

"Oh, what a gentleman you are!" She leaned against him and sighed with exaggerated relief, almost burying her face in his shirt. "To think what might have happened to me if you had not been here to catch me!"

"I'm glad to be of assistance."

"Do you think, Jay, that you could . . . that someday, you might consider taking care of me . . . forever?"

Jay dropped his eyes, a bur of discomfort chafing his mind. "Yes, but . . . I'm not worthy of you . . . or anyone else."

She laughed musically. "That's just one man's opinion."

"I . . . haven't a lovely past. One black spot mars my otherwise passable record."

"Oh, pooh, nobody is perfect," she brushed away his moment of contemplation. "We all have a black spot or two on the ledger of our lives. I say forget it and have yourself a grand old time."

"But mine is bad," he persisted. "I committed a crime several years ago—a crime akin to murder."

"No sin is worse than another. It wouldn't bother me one iota what you did in the past. I live for the present, with no thought of morbid bygones." She stopped and looked into his guileless eyes. "Oh, I'm so glad you will love and protect me. I've really had no one all my life, you know. Granny Myrt tried her best, but she always . . . *resented* me."

Only when he left Myrt's house and headed for the Harris homestead did Jay hit the ground. A python-like panic squeezed his heart. What had he done? *Why, I hardly know the girl,* he told himself, *and what did I get myself into? Is she a Christian? The only mention she made of God was a "walk in His creation." I must have taken leave of my senses; I have certainly acted a fool in encouraging the girl's friendship without consulting with the Harrises. What had she said about borrowing Mr. Harris's boat for a joy ride? Surely she didn't mean on Sunday!* Jay sighed wearily at the tangle of unanswered questions brought on by an afternoon spent in Molly Rushing's company.

Molly basked in her victory. "Granny Myrt!" she danced about her grandmother's cottage gleefully, impishly. "I snared that handsome brute! He's promised to marry me. He promised this very day! Why, he was a pushover! You'd better start planning for my wedding . . ."

Word traveled fast.

Molly told Myrt, and Myrt told her pastor. Brother Stevens stroked his chin and looked troubled. "I'm . . . not sure it's for the best, Sister Myrt . . ."

Myrt misinterpreted the frown lines between his bushy gray eyebrows.

"Of course Molly has strayed, pastor, but most o' us sowed some tares in our youth, too," she hastened to remind him.

"Oh, it's not that I hold Molly in question," he hurried to explain, "I just . . . I just wondered if she knew the young man well enough . . . ah, for *marriage.*"

"I realize it is quite sudden-like, pastor, but we had 'im in our home, an' he seems a true gentleman indeed. Real refined. Better'n most she's set her cap on in th' past. I'm mighty pleased."

"Certainly. Certainly. But . . ."

"But what, pastor? Is there some skeleton in the closet that we should know about. He isn't divorced, is he?" Her faded hazel eyes grew grave with the deplorable thought.

"Oh, no, I didn't mean anything like that, Sister Myrt. It's just that young Brother Walls doesn't . . . ah, exactly embrace our doctrine."

"What doctrine?"

"He believes there's only one God, and we believe there are three persons in the Godhead." Pastor Stevens loathed doctrinal discussions and doubly so with women.

"Three persons?"

"Yes, Sister Myrt. I've directed many messages on this subject. There's the Father, the Son, and the Holy Ghost, three separate and distinct persons."

"But Jesus said, 'I and my Father are one.' That's over in John 10."

"He meant one in purpose."

"Why didn't He say so then? Anyway, He told Philip in chapter 14, 'When you've seen Me, you've seen th' Father.' "

The parson steered the subject another direction. "Jay didn't have the same baptismal words said over him that we say."

"What did he have said?"

"Just in the name of Jesus."

"What's wrong with that? That sounds good enough to me."

"He didn't get all three."

"I'm thinkin' he did get all three in one. Somewhere it says do ever'thing we do in word er deed in that name," defended Myrt. "Anyhow, Brother Stevens, Molly wouldn't give a care if'n he was a' infidel so long's as he's a man an' good-lookin'. An' I'll stand b'hind 'er in this un cause I *like* 'im. An' I'll expect you, as my pastor, to say th' ceremony!" She left him staring after her. She had never stood up to her pastor before.

And word got back to Martha Harris that Jay was engaged to be married to Molly Rushing.

Chapter Eleven

Outer Storm, Inner Storm

My boat is gone! What will I do now?

Sally sank down on the shale-strewn river bank, willing herself to find a solution. Her exhausted mind took the new disappointment at twice its weight.

Dust and litter scrambled along the river's edge, driven by an impatient wind. The boathouses groaned. Smell of rain brought her to her feet. With one frantic glance at the dark, turgid sky, she realized that a storm was upon her!

A powerful gust that seemed caught in a fit of anger almost tore the satchel from her grasp as she hurried, running to find shelter. By the time she reached the town's main street again, sheets of blinding rain sent water flowing along the gutters in rushing tides. She flattened herself against a building, borrowing protection from its overhang. Shutters banged, and signs squeaked errily on their rusty hinges.

Amidst the majestic thunder of the heavens, the cheap earthy music of a jukebox floated from somewhere nearby. Vague food smells wafted from a late night cafe where night revelers wined and dined, giving no heed to the boiling elements. A spasm of hunger gripped Sally, sending a nauseous weakness; supper seemed a forgotten dream. Then without warning, the wind changed directions, sending the deluge toward Sally.

She inched her way cautiously along the weathered building until she reached a porch-like opening. Shivering, she plunged under its roof, grateful for a temporary refuge.

She had not been there long when she heard a familiar voice. "Why, there's my girlie, Monroe! Ain't that our mermaid? And she's might near drowned!"

"Believe 'tis, awright!"

"Les go rescue that baby . . ."

"You get her and bring her to dansh for the boys." The words came thick and slurred. "Shay, fellows! We're fixing to have shum *show*. Did ya ever shee a mermaid *dansh?*"

Sally clamped one hand over her mouth to keep from screaming and, dropping her gripsack, placed her other hand on her heart which beat so wildly it seemed to hurt. "Please God, don't let me faint!" she prayed fiercely, urging her feet to flee from this dread new awfulness. *Am I actually running, or am I standing still?* she wondered in her confusion.

"Why, sheez gone! Youz jesh having vishons from too mush . . . hic . . . shweet milk . . . ha, ha, ha!" The sickening words followed Sally as she vanished into the relentless torrent, oblivious of the downpour slapping her face, mingling with her tears.

I left my travel case! How rash she had been to go out at night alone, she chided herself. *But I will not go back for it!* Sally would have been filled with revulsion could she have seen the shameless men in their stupor of alcohol going through her personal items, leering and making base remarks.

Even the tiny excuse of a room at Mrs. Gordon's would be a welcome sanctuary from the raging skies tonight. She forged on, ignoring her soggy clothing and oozing stockings. Just as she reached the rooming house, the rain stopped as quickly as it came, leaving a heavy fog thick in the inlet.

Spent and drenched, Sally pulled herself up the short steps to the front entrance, eagerly grasping the door-knob. The door was locked.

Numb with despair, she sat on the splintered stoop and wept bitterly—childlike—for some time. Then, an idea struck her befuddled mind. Gathering her sodden skirt about her, she ventured to the alley with the hopes of gaining entrance through her bedroom window. The stench of spoiled refuse turned her uneasy stomach. A large rodent, startled by the movement, tumbled from his haven of debris and ran carelessly over her foot. It was too much; Sally screamed involuntarily before she could get her hand to her mouth.

A boarder in a room above put on his gas light. Sally stole away posthaste, quailing at the thought of being discovered here, giving a fleeting glance toward her room window above. It was too high to negotiate anyhow.

Sally felt she had reached her extremity. "Just let

me die, God," she whispered wretchedly into the midnight blackness. However, another thought followed on the heels of that one. *But God, I'm not ready to die! I've sinned against You and I've sinned against home! Oh, please forgive my foolishness! I've been rebellious and disobedient.* Sally began to sob, her repentant heart reaching toward God. *I have hurt Mama and Papa, and I have hurt You. Only take me back to You and to my home and I'll make it up to You and my family.*

The tears and prayers went on into the night, and though nothing changed externally, something changed inside. Sally's burden lightened.

She found mossy sward behind a squatty shrub and sat down. She pulled her knees up tight against her damp body, and in this ball-like position she fell asleep, wondering vaguely who would remove the bread blanket from the rising breakfast rolls.

The rattling milk wagon awoke her as it made its busy predawn rounds. With considerable effort, she straightened out her coiled body. When Mrs. Gordon unbuttoned the door to retrieve the milk, leaving it open to catch the heavy morning air, Sally stole in and to her quarters. She changed to dry garments quickly, pinned her hair into a tight chignon, and hurried to the kitchen, feeling stiff and waterlogged.

Mrs. Gordon, already frying the salt pork, glanced at her reproachfully. She said nothing, however, probably not wishing to risk the loss of this new cook who made her smorgasboard the most desirable eating place in town, with a growing clientele.

In a daze, Sally moved about sick and sore. Because of her early morning heart-talk with God, she remained pleasant, not slacking in her food preparation though she ate little herself. She prayed for strength to endure the arduous day.

When the last pan of greasy dishwater had been dashed out the back door and the leftovers stored in the larder, Sally dragged herself to her dismal little room, her head dizzy and aching. Her mind and body took its revenge. She fell asleep, fully clothed, to the montonous droning of a cricket under her gray cot.

The cresting sun sent its stippled rays splashing across a drying earth into Sally's room—and still she slept. Mrs. Gordon, her patience with the girl nearly gone, found her thus. "Harriet!" she reprimanded, shaking her awake. "I will not tolerate laziness! This is the second morning you have overslept. I cannot furnish room and board free to someone who will not get up and work!"

Sally opened her eyes in alarm. She tried to speak, but a dry croak came from her miserable throat. She gestured toward her throat and head.

"If you are pretending illness to get out of work, Harriet . . ."

Sally shook her head vigorously, tears forming.

"Unless things go better than this tomorrow, you'd best look for lodging elsewhere." Mrs. Gordon stalked from the room and went to the kitchen to start a greasy, tasteless meal for her boarders. Of course, there would be a volley of complaints about the food; some of her more fastidious tenants might even threaten to check out.

This startling new apprehension of being turned out took Sally to her knees to croak out a broken prayer. "Dear Jesus," she prayed desperately, "If I am to be turned out on the street, what am I to do? Please make me well enough to stand on my feet and work tomorrow." She paused. "Really, God, my life isn't mine to choose anymore. I gave it to You a few hours ago. You do it Your way." She drew a long, deep breath of surrender then crawled back onto the uncomfortable cot and fell into a deep and merciful slumber.

A chaotic day began for Mrs. Gordon. Her mediocre biscuits failed to rise; she forgot the saleratus. Her gravy lumped into a pasty mass that resembled dumplings while she minded the eggs that nonetheless scrambled themselves into hard knots. Meeting failure at every turn, she proved equally as disagreeable as her poorly prepared food. Repeatedly she answered the detestable question, "Where is our pretty cook who usually serves us good meals?" It did nothing for her ego.

She had threatened to dismiss "Harriet." But the disastrous day proved that she could not do without the girl's culinary arts and cheerful smile and keep her tenants happy.

And of all days for the telephone executive, Mr. Cotterby, to show up for room service! Mrs. Gordon had no time for an appealing tray arrangement, and when she returned for his dishes, he had touched little of the colorless food—and left no tip at all. She heard him inquiring of other residents where the "little lady with the golden hair" had taken herself.

When Mrs. Gordon, dragging the heels of her shoddy shoes worn down to a rakish angle, stacked the last greasy plate from the evening meal in the dishpan and looked at the monumental stack, she was obliged to hire a girl to finish up for her. She paid an enormous sum for the help. In a few short days, she had quite forgotten how much energy it took to manage a single day's work at her inn.

The following morning, Sally was in the kitchen kneading light bread when Mrs. Gordon brought in the milk left on the front steps by the milkman. She hummed a church song and greeted her waspish boss with a congenial smile. The corners of Mrs. Gordon's mouth refused to turn up.

"I'm sorry I wasn't able to help yesterday." Sally's apology was sincere.

"So am I," snapped Mrs. Gordon peevishly. "I had to hire a girl to clean up the supper dishes. She charged me an arm and a leg."

"I hope I won't have to miss work anymore." Sally's hands toiled on, held to her task by sheer necessity, as she rolled out her crust for the tasty fruit tarts that her "customers" loved and put the coffee on to boil.

The sun came out to steam press the earth, bringing a sultry morning that seemed unusually long. But throughout those long hours, Sally did her utmost to please Mrs. Gordon. Yet there seemed no limits to her employer's demands. In fact, it seemed to be the taskmaster's design to extract the last ounce of strength from Sally, giving as little as possible in return.

Mrs. Gordon had a visitor that day. Sally caught sketches of the conversation as she passed from kitchen to dining area. The voice of the guest rose and fell pleasantly, while Mrs. Gordon's voice sounded piqued.

"I would like to talk to . . ." the pleasant voice trailed off, lost among other sounds.

"Harriet . . . homeless waif . . . I'm supporting her with my own . . ." the unpleasant voice spoke.

". . . are you paying her, Mrs. Gordon?"

". . . none of your business. I'm paying her *top wages.*"

". . . offer her a good job."

"She wouldn't be interested in working anywhere else. She loves her work here . . . is content . . . loves me."

". . . heard of her cooking abilities . . . need her . . . will make her an offer . . ."

"No. . . . is like my own daughter . . . loves working for me . . . would not leave me for any amount of money . . ."

Sally stood rooted, a platter in each hand. Why, someone had come to offer her a job that would bring her *money.* She could save enough to return home. And Mrs. Gordon persisted in destroying her chances of ever getting a paying job. Jail! That's what this place was. A prison for both her soul and body! How could she ever hope to escape? She could not even hope for a postage stamp to send a letter for deliverance!

Blackness reached out for her. Then a light. *Remember, Sally,* a still voice whispered in her mind. *You belong to Your Heavenly Father, and it doesn't require a postage stamp to get a message to Him.*

Chapter Twelve

A Surprise Visit

"*M*yrt said Molly sent word she'd be in th' weekend an' to tell you she would be expectin' you to take 'er on a boat floatin' Sunday," Martha informed Jay, relaying the message unwillingly, but dutifully.

"I . . . I'm afraid I'll have to disappoint her. I don't pleasure ride on the Lord's Day."

"Oh, she'd be displeased if'n you b'gin spurnin' 'er suggestions right off at th' start."

"At the start of what, Mrs. Harris?"

"At th' startin' o' yore betrothin'."

"But I'm not betrothed to Molly . . . or anyone else."

"Molly said you was. She told 'er gran'ma that you a'ready promised to take good keer o' her fer life. Didn't you?"

"Well . . . yes, I mean no . . . I don't *think* I made any promises in regards to getting married. I told her I would want to marry someday, but I didn't tell her that I would wed *her*. Why, I really don't even know the young lady. I've never seen her but once!"

"No, you shore don't know 'er er else you wouldn't get yoreself tangled with 'er."

"Did she say I promised to *marry* her?"

"Why, yes, I b'lieve she did. An' right away, too. Sister Myrt a'ready talked to Parson Stevens 'bout performin' th' ceremony fer you an' Molly."

"I . . . something isn't right, Mrs. Harris."

"She'll hold yer feet to th' fire if'n you made any kind o' commitment, willin' er not."

"I *hope* I didn't say anything that could be interpreted as a commitment."

"It'll be her word a'gin yor'n. An' her word can be mighty stiff. She'll make you look mighty poorly an' have you on th' witness stand fer breach o' promise. I'm mighty sorry fer you if'n you opened yore mouth in 'er presence."

Henry walked into the room in time to observe Jay's perplexed frown. "What's th' problem, friend?"

"Molly proposed that I take her on a river float in your boat come Sunday and I . . ."

"I don't have a boat."

"Why, Henry, we have th' old floater William built an' named *River Rat,*" Martha reminded in a scolding tone.

"The boat is gone, Martha. Only a stub o' rope tied to th' cottonwood is all that's left o' Will's boat. Somebody took 'er, er else she yanked loose in a storm an' floated away on 'er own."

"How long ago was it you noticed it gone?" Martha questioned.

"'Bout a month. Right 'bout th' time Jay came along."

"Couldn't'a been no storm, Henry. We ain't had no storms bad 'nough to warsh away anything in two er three months—not since afore school let out fer th' summer."

"Th' boat ain't really no great loss, Martha. We have no need fer it nohow since th' boys er all gone off. They enjoyed it fer fishin'. Warn't good fer much else. I do my fishin' from th' bank er trot line." He turned to Jay. "I'd be glad fer you to have used it anytime, if'n it was to home."

"I really didn't want to take the girl on a float anyhow," Jay responded, rather flatly.

"She's tryin' to trap 'im up, Henry. What'd I tell you? She's got Myrt b'lievin' Jay is gonna marry 'er," Martha's voice rankled with irritation.

"I'm guessin' he don't have to marry nobody he don't want to, Martha."

"It 'mounts to more'n that, Henry."

Jay sat pondering his predicament. The distressful thing was that he couldn't remember what he actually did say to Molly Rushing. Had he promised to marry her in an egotistical moment—or hadn't he?

"What happened? Did *she* ask you to marry *her*, Jay?" Henry chuckled.

"I guess that's what it amounted to, Mr. Harris, if there was a proposal made. For I surely didn't ask *her*. Not on purpose, anyhow!"

"And did you consent?" Henry's eyes twinkled. Martha cast him a dark brown look for making a joke of such a weighty matter, but Henry ignored her.

"I didn't realize I was consenting to a permanent relationship, but I may have. I . . . don't remember what I *did* say. I'm . . . not accustomed to female pitfalls I'm afraid. You might say I'm smarting, but smarter."

Henry laughed again in spite of Martha's scowl. "You picked a bad one to learn on."

"If you will excuse me, I'll pray about it." Jay got up and went to his room, closing the door behind him.

"I'd be 'shamed fer treatin' his problem so light-hearted, Henry," Martha reproached. "The boy's right troubled in his mind."

"Yore right, Martha. An' I guess he's got a right to be."

On Sunday, Jay stayed home with his Bible. The thoughts of another encounter with the beautiful, black-haired temptress brought a recoil from his soul. The answer to his dilemma seemed just out of his grasp, and until he came to some decision in handling the sticky situation, he chose to worship alone.

Molly, alluringly dressed in a new and fashionable faille suit, sat primly on the Harris pew, awaiting her "prospective husband." The notes of the wheezy organ sounded the services's initiation as Henry and Martha entered the chapel, unsmiling and solemn. Molly glanced about eagerly for Jay—and when he did not appear, she fidgeted, turned her head to look toward the rear entrance, then fidgeted some more. Finally, she got up and walked out.

Jay, lost in Bible reading, heard the warning bark that Patches used to announce a visitor. Then the knock came, at first lightly, then becoming more pronounced. He was almost to the front door before he recognized that it was Molly. Her glossy black hair, shaped into a stylish upsweep, ended in a comb-secured pompadour.

"Hi!" she chirped flippantly, "May I come in?"

"I'm . . . sorry, but I feel it isn't proper to invite a young lady in when there is no one here but me, a lone man."

Molly's great painted eyes widened in disbelief. Then she threw back her proud head and laughed merrily. "Oh, the likes of you. I won't hurt you!"

"And besides, this home doesn't belong to me, and I've no right to invite guests into the Harris home without consulting them first."

"Why, they won't care! They've known me all my life. I'm a good friend of their daughter's."

"I have rules for myself, and I will not break them."

"I really didn't want to come in anyhow." Her eyes held a mocking jest, as she edged closer to the separating screen. "I'm ready to go on the boat ride you promised me."

"I have scruples against joy riding on the Lord's Day, Miss Rushing. Grandmother instilled them in me."

"Oh, pooh. That's antediluvian!" Molly tried her favorite analogue on Jay.

"I don't know where I'd find a boat even if I wasn't so . . . antediluvian."

Molly took the statement as a weakening of Jay's will. "Mr. Harris has a boat."

"Mr. Harris *did* have a boat at one time. But it has been missing for a month now."

"A likely story."

"Excuse me, please, Miss Rushing. I was having my private devotion when you disturbed me."

"Miss Rushing, pooh. Call me Molly like a fiance should."

"I repeat. Excuse me, Miss Rushing. God and I are very busy."

Molly, unaccustomed to the rebuff of any man, drew herself up indignantly. "You're not backing out on your pledge, Mr. Walls. That wouldn't be *Christian*. You did promise to marry me someday," she reminded in a jaded tone.

"I did?"

"Now don't pretend amnesia, dear. I've already announced our wedding plans. Granny Myrt wants us to say our vows right here at my home church. Then we can go away anywhere—the farther from here the better!"

"May we discuss it later, Miss Rushing? Right now, I want some time alone with the Lord."

Jay stealthily latched the screen so that she could not force her way into the sitting room. Then he turned and walked away without another word.

On the ottoman with his elbows on his knees and his chin resting on his fist, he pondered this new complication. *I'll either have to marry the girl to save my dignity in this place,* he calculated to himself, *or clear out—and I'll choose the latter. It's knapsack time again. I can't go to The Springs for work now.*

Over Martha's cornpone and pinto beans, Henry commented, "Molly brung 'erself to church this mornin', lookin' all daisy-fresh. First time since she was in pigtails that she's been *two* Sundays in a row."

"An' when she seen you warn't there, she jest up an' left!" Martha finished, directing her remarks to Jay.

"Yes, she came here." Jay dropped his eyes in embarrassment.

"Molly Rushing came *here?*" Martha exploded.

"Lookin' fer you?"

"Yes, ma'am. I latched the screen door so she couldn't get in and kidnap me." He grinned, but his face lacked color.

"Well, fer th' life o' me . . ."

"I've had to make some decisions this morning." Jay lifted his clear brown eyes—and a tear could almost be seen. "A decision that will change my life's plans."

"I hope you decided not to marry Molly Rushin'!"

"That's right. And I'll be moving on to another part of the country tomorrow."

Martha paled. Henry pushed back his chair in a gesture of tired resignation.

"Will . . . my leaving inconvenience you, Mr. Harris? You've been good to me, and I don't want to leave you in a lurch regardless of my own personal . . . wishes."

"I . . . if you could find it in yore heart to stay on jest one more week an' help me hoe th' cotton crop in th' big south field, I'd be ferever grateful. You could be gone by th' Sunday next an' escape Molly."

"I'll be more than glad to help you, Mr. Harris. Do you think we can whip it out in one week?"

"I b'lieve we can if we stay with it an' work hard. But 'tain't fair askin' . . ."

Jay waved away Henry's misgivings. "I've no destination, so another week won't matter in the least, Mr. Harris."

Martha, ready to cry, turned her face away. "That girl's caused me nuthin' but heartache an' grief," she blurted, hurting with each bitter word. "She might nigh lost us one o' our own boys, she tried to backslide our Sally, an' now she's took Jay away from us!"

103

"Mrs. Harris, please don't grieve. Molly isn't . . . the only reason I'm moving on. There's other things . . ."

"I 'low she's th' reason you're movin' on so quick-like."

"Perhaps. But since the first day I came, I have been considering a move to some other location."

"Have we . . . not treated you square, boy?" Henry asked, anguished.

"Oh, Mr. Harris! Don't ever entertain that thought!" Jay urged hastily, realizing how Henry had mistaken his statement. "You and Mrs. Harris have been only *too* good to me. And that's where the problem lies."

"I . . . don't understand."

"I have a great . . . sin in my past life that, if you knew, I'm sure you would not want me around another minute."

"Don't say it!" erupted Martha. "Whatever you done, I'm shore you done made it right with God. An' if'n He forgave you, then 'twould be no problem fer me an' Henry. Ain't that right, Henry?"

Jay laid aside his fork. "I had just turned fourteen when I committed the . . . crime. Grandmother had her first bad spell, and I was terribly frightened for her, wondering what would happen to me if she should die. We hadn't much money; I had been working hit and miss on the railroad helping a crosstie boss and making a pitiful child's wage—not nearly enough to buy Grandmother's medicine and pay the doctor bill.

"Then the town bully came along, several years older than me, a giant of a boy. He offered me a heap of money—pay dirt he called it—to go along with him on one of his 'hauls.' He promised me a whopping five hundred dollars to be his accomplice. I didn't ask what the job was; I simply said I would go, knowing that the money would get Grandmother into the hospital where she could get well. In my adolescent mind, I considered this an answer straight from heaven. Instead, it was an invitation from the devil himself.

"The rascal I went along with had a vicious temper! I tried to act tough and curse right along with him; inside I ran scared and guilt-ridden.

"The crime we committed to get the money resulted in a girl's death. An armed officer shot at me, barely missing. Sometimes I think death would have been better than the conscience I've had to live with these past eleven or so years. But we escaped with our lives. We didn't get the 'paydirt.'

"The other man is in prison for the holdup, but I wanted no part of that sort of life. We parted ways, and I didn't tell Grandmother—or anyone—what I had done. I'm telling it now to the first human, although Patches knows the story by heart. It would have brought my dear grandmother to her grave to know that I had a part in injuring anyone . . . and I would have had her blood on my hands too. Sin . . . is a terrible thing, Mr. Harris. It never stops . . . hurting."

Moved to tears, Martha pleaded, "Don't feel like you gotta leave on account o' that a'ready forgiven wrong, Jay. That's all in th' past."

"I've heard that if a relative of the dead innocent finds me, he will turn me in to the law yet."

"We'll stand fer you, Jay. You don't have to be afeared here," Henry vowed vehemently. "I know th' sheriff personally, an' we'll explain it all to 'im an' have it taken from your life ferever."

"I'll stay on and help you this next week, Mr. Harris."

A small flower-scented note came by post for Jay that week. It was so personal, so intimate that he blushed. It further convinced him that his exit must be permanent. It was signed, "Your future wife, Molly Rushing."

New Fears

"*W*ill you be in these parts long?" the old lady asked pointedly. Her hair reminded Sally of the powdered wig her great-grandfather wore in his wedding portrait.

"I . . . don't know."

"You are new here, aren't you?"

"Yes, ma'am."

"Do you like working here?"

Sally looked at the woman tiredly. "It's a job—food and lodging, anyhow."

"What's your name, miss? And where do you hail from?"

"Sal . . . Harriet."

"Um. Sal from Harriet. Now I never heard of that place. A long piece off I suppose?"

"Yes, ma'am."

"Sal. That's a wee bit of a name. But then you're a

107

wee bit of a girlie, so I guess it suits you."

Sally didn't bother to correct her.

"My name's Gracie. Gracie Lindsay."

"I see."

"Well, why don't you have a little sid'down, girlie. Since you're here, you need to know something of our shadowy past." The aged soul nodded toward a tattered cane-bottom chair, some of its limp bamboo hanging.

"Please excuse me, Mrs. Lindsay. But I haven't time to sit today," Sally returned as she hurried the mop over the oil-caked floor.

"Then I'll just give you your learning while you work!"

Sally said nothing; her mood precluded trifling conversation. The weight in her heart scarcely allowed her to move about, making no allowances for the effort of talking.

"Right here where this very boarding house sits— yes, right on this very spot—was the scene of a terrible Indian raid. My mind's not too good on dates, but I believe it was back in '46. Anyhow, it was the year before Mr. Ross started ferrying people across the Brazos River. Sydney P. that was. I'll never forget Sydney P. A real pioneer he was.

"Anyhow . . . now what was I saying. Oh, yes. Right here where this boarding house sits was where my aunt and uncle on my mother's side of the family was massacred. Oh, it was awful. Yes, right here.

"And as I was saying, when Sydney started the ferry up, families started moving in from all over *everywhere*. They came in *swarms*. My family came along, too, of course. That's why I'm here, you see. And we were mighty glad to see that bridge built across the great Brazos River back in '70. That's been thirty years ago, hasn't it? Now that's when Waco really began to boom. Do you know where Waco got its name, girlie?"

"No, ma'am." Sally hurried anxious to escape the unsolicited history lesson. Even in school, history had never been her favorite subject.

"Well, it was from the Huecho Indians who lived here years and years ago. Huecho does sound a bit like Waco, don't you think?"

Sally nodded absently.

"You do look a bit peaked, child. I don't think the missus would mind you resting for a few minutes . . ."

"I have other rooms to finish before dinner."

"Well, you are a determined one. Mrs. Gordon's lucky to get you. But as I was saying . . . now what was I saying? Do you know anything about Indian raids, girlie?"

"Only what Miss—only what I learned in school."

"Back a half century ago, everybody lived close to the edge of life so to speak. I guess it was kind of bad of the white man to take the land from the red man. Mother always said you can't slice nothing thin enough to just have one side. But lawsy me, those Indians were plumb *cruel* . . ."

Sally moved to the window for air; the room seemed suddenly smaller.

"My grandpa wore a six-shooter like he'd take a cold if he took it off. Even slept with it. But that gun saved grandpa's life more than once . . . and lost some other lives in the process.

"Now what was I saying? Well, back to the Indians. There was lots of raiding parties along this Brazos River.

Most of them took place in the dark of the night or about dawn. If you lived out alone or in a tiny settlement, you were earmarked for a raid for sure.

"Those Texas reds were hit-and-run warriors, too. They planned well, hit full force, killed, scalped, and burned."

Sally, her knees weak now, pulled at the soiled muslin sheets, willing her hands to the work of changing the bed.

"Now what was I saying? Oh, I wanted to tell you the story of my father's kin who lived down near Round Mountain, south and west of here. That's where we lived before we moved here.

"Old Tom liked to fish and so did his wife Mary. On a real hot day in July or August—I remember the year was '73 not long after we had settled here—they caught up their poles and told their kids to stay home with their grandma, Mary's mother.

"Tom and Mary was in a right gladsome mood that day, trudging down to Cypress Creek. Mary started right away catching some nice catfish on the dough balls she'd made, and it was just like a nice holiday. They laughed and talked like a couple of young spooners.

"Tom moved down river to fish, never giving troubles no mind. All of a sudden Mary screamed. A blood-curdling scream it was. A painted Indian stood across the little stream grinning at her. Mary dropped her pole and started to run, but she didn't get far. She was shot about waist high.

"Tom was but about forty yards away, sitting on a big rock outcropping to fish. He heard Mary's scream and ran to her. He didn't have a gun—nothing but his pole, which wouldn't do one bit of good, of course.

"As Tom ran for help, he was shot, too. Right in the head. Both of them were scalped. Tom lost his good shoes, and those heedless raiders carried away the whole stringer of catfish!

"But back to . . . now what was I saying? Oh, yes . . . my aunt and uncle who died *right here*. They had a wee lassie, still in the cradle. Everybody in the whole settlement was killed but the wee baby girl. The Indians took the child—she had bright red hair—and reared her in their tribal customs. Poor darling never realized that she wasn't a redskin. She grew up and married one of the young chiefs and . . ."

"I hope your room is suitable, Mrs. Lindsay. If not, please be so kind as to register your complaint with me rather than with Mrs. Gordon."

"Oh, I think it looks quite fine, girlie. Of course, my eyesight is not as good as it used to be when . . ."

"I beg to bid you a good day."

"Well, girlie, they say the Indian raids are over in this part of the world, but I wouldn't count on it. Father always said they would put up one last terrible fight, and that it would be the worst in the history of America. And I wouldn't be surprised if he's not right about that. You know, girlie, I go to sleep every night thinking this may be the very night it will happen again just like it did a half century ago. History repeats itself, they say. The nights are getting darker, you know . . ."

The old lady felt at her neckline for her brooch, and finding it missing, looked down to her lap in search of it. "But tell me about yourself, girlie. This place called Harriet. Is it a big place? Were you born there?" She looked up and blinked her watery eyes. "Well, why did the girlie leave so fast?"

Sally had fled, her heart churning with a mixture of dread and anxiety.

Chapter Fourteen

Change of Plans

"*T*h' new talkin' machine is put in!"

Martha pushed the apple pies to the back of the warming oven, keeping one eye on them and the other on the steaming kettle of egg noodles.

"Has it rung yet?" Henry buried his face in the clean towel on the roller, streaking it with field dirt.

"Yep. Th' phone comp'ny called to make shore th' ring was goin' to sound."

"I meant have you been gossipin' on it yet?"

"Nobody knows we got it."

"What's our ring?"

"Two longs an' one short."

"A party line."

"What's that?"

"That's where you can pick up th' horn an' hear other people talkin' 'bout you." Henry winked at Jay who awaited his turn at the wash basin.

"I don't have time fer that, Henry."

"We'll see. What's our number?"

"58-J."

"That's easy to remember since it's my age this year."

"An' it'll be mine in five more year."

"Well, why don't you call Sarah an' say hello?"

"I'll do that after supper." She turned out the buttered field peas.

"After supper is a mighty busy time fer telephone lines," Henry hazed. "You might have to keep clickin' th' lines to ever get a chance to call somebody yoreself. Even clickin' don't always work."

Martha turned to Jay, reciting the proposal she had planned all day. "If'n you'll stay on with us, I'll han'le that Molly Rushing fer you . . ."

"No, Mrs. Harris. I thank you for your offer, but I'm afraid that would make trouble for everyone. I'll slip out quietly . . . and just tell Molly I left . . . and left no forwarding address. Someday . . . I'll stop back by for a visit to my favorite people."

Martha's plan had failed.

"It's but two more days till Jay leaves us," Martha grieved to Henry that night. "I've said ever'thing I know to keep 'im with us. Th' house is gonna be cryin' with lonesome when he's gone away."

"Wished 'twas jest th' house to be cryin'. I'm afeared 'twill be you cryin', too, Martha."

"He seems so like one o' our'n, Henry."

"But we can't hold 'im, Martha. I told you from th' start that 'is stay was only fer tempor'ry an' he'd itch to move on someday. He's been a mighty big blessin' to our bruised hearts these few weeks. We can thank God fer that.''

Martha sighed. ''Women's hearts git bigger holes in 'um when some'un's missin' from th' table than men's does.''

''I dunno 'bout that, Martha. Men hurt deep an' have to act brave to hold up ever'body else.''

After much fretting, Martha fell asleep, forgetting the ''talking machine'' or the call to Sarah. And when the telephone jangled as she slept Friday morning, she jumped nervously. The bed beside her was empty; Henry and Jay had slipped out early.

The call came from Sarah.

''You might nigh scared me out o' my wits!'' Martha told her.

''How so, Mama?''

''I fergot 'bout th' machine, an' I ain't used to noises—'ceptin' th' rooster—when I'm sleepin'.''

''Have you er Papa read th' paper this mornin', Mama?''

''Land no, child. I ain't but jest got up. An' yore Paw's tryin' to whip out th' hoein' whiles he's got Jay. Why?''

''There's a piece in there 'bout a lost girl in Ft. Worth.''

''Reckon it could be our Sally, Sarah?''

''I hope not, Mama. The girl was . . . killed this week.''

''What does it say, Sarah, quick!'' The earpiece shook in Martha's hand; she dropped down in the spider rocker.

''Mama, I don't want to tell you over th' phone. I don't want you to go faintin'. An' I can't come over there with these babies o' mine asleep right now.''

''I promise, Sarah, I won't pass out. Wait. Lemme

git me a cold rag." The telephone went silent.

"Now, Sarah."

"Th' piece kind of describes what Sally looks like. It says a girl was found on North Belnap Street in th' alley behind a nightclub. They couldn't tell what er who killed 'er. They're still searchin' fer clues an' suspects. She had long blond hair an' blue eyes an' was wearin' a blue mornin' gown. Th' county is buryin' her body today, seein' nobody came to claim 'er."

"Jest a minnet, Sarah." Martha daubed her face and neck with the cloth. "Thank you fer callin'. I'll take th' paper to th' south field an' find yore Papa. It's . . . it sounds like our Sally . . . my baby Sally . . ." A sob choked her words off, and she replaced the receiver in its cradle, her heart fluttering like a cup towel on the clothesline tormented by a fickle wind.

She snatched up the *Fort Worth Telegram* and stumbled toward the field to find Henry. In sight of the workers, she lurched and toppled to the ground. Jay saw her fall.

"Mr. Harris!" he cried out. "Here comes your wife with something in her hand, but she has fallen."

Henry ran to Martha, who simply held out the newspaper, a wild look in her eyes. "What is it, Martha?" he coaxed.

"Let's get her to the house, Mr. Harris," Jay urged. "And then perhaps she can tell us what the problem is."

Wedging her between them, the two men supported Martha back to the house. She pointed to the telephone and said, "Sarah."

"Somethin's happened to one o' Sarah's bunch, Jay," Henry explained. "I'll ring 'er."

The line was taken by Henry's detested "gossipers" talking about the price of eggs. "Please," he interrupted curtly, "this is a' emergency. I *must* have th' line at once. You can have it back all th' rest o' th' day when I'm done callin' my daughter." They released the line with a sharp click.

"Operator! Please connect me with 43-J immediately!" Henry yelled at the telephone, and then forgot to wait for Sarah to answer. "Sarah," he began before the connection was completed, "Maw said fer me to call you." Henry heard telephones picked up to listen all along the line. It profoundly annoyed him.

"Yes, Papa?"

"Maw said I was to call . . ."

"It's about th' piece in th' newspaper, Papa. 'Bout a girl bein' killed in Fort Worth. Fits th' description o' Sally." Henry heard gasps along the line.

"Thank you, Sarah." Henry wished the neighbors to know no more. By noon the news would have swept the community like a recalcitrant forest fire.

"Hand me the newspaper, Jay."

Henry found the front page item and read it to Martha who wailed shamelessly. He turned to Jay, remembering that they had not discussed their prodigal daughter with the young man. "It's our daughter, we're afeared. Her name's Sally an' she left jest afore you came along. 'Bout a day afore, in fact. Makes it hard on th' wife, since she's our youngest . . . th' last."

"Could you give me a description of your daughter, Mr. Harris?"

"Well, th' paper purty well says it like she was. She had long hair to her waist, never touched by shears . . .

kinda gold colored. Th' color came through from my maw's side o' th' family. She was medium tall an' a bit too thinish. She had blue eyes . . ."

"Henry, why don't you jest show Sally's pitcher to Jay. It's on my bureau in our room, on th' side by the winder. Oh, my baby!"

Henry brought the tintype and handed it to Jay.

Jay looked at it, taken aback. *This is the girl I saw floating down the river!* he thought. *And she wasn't headed for Forth Worth!*

"I . . . I don't believe this is the girl the newspaper is talking about," he stammered, not knowing how to convey his knowledge to them without exposing his secret, and hers.

Martha stopped wailing and looked at Jay, surprised. "Why not?" she wiped her eyes and nose with a kerchief from her apron pocket.

"I . . . saw this girl . . . once . . ."

"See, Jay seen her. She ain't dead," triumphed Henry, grasping the vestage of hope.

"He mighta seen her afore she died, Henry." Martha's common-sense statement dashed his optimism.

"Where was she when you seen her, Jay?" he asked.

"She was nowhere *near* Fort Worth, Mr. Harris. She was . . . west of here. She is the most beautiful young lady I have ever seen."

"That's our Sally-girl, awright. Did you make acquaintance with 'er?"

"No, I just saw her in passing. As far as I know, she didn't even see me. But I'm sure that the girl in this picture is the girl I saw. And I'm sure she's . . . not the girl . . . that was killed."

118

"Do you think you could go back . . . west . . . where you seen 'er . . . an' find 'er again?"

"With time, yes. I believe I could find her."

"Would you do it fer us, Jay, afore you leave us?" Martha leaped from her chair in her excitement. "We'd be ferever obliged to you!"

"I'd furnish th' money fer yer search," prompted Henry humbly. "All th' money you'd need fer however long it took."

"I don't want any money, Mr. Harris. I've saved what you've paid me for the farm help, and I'll be glad to go at my own expense. I owe you a deep debt anyhow. I'll go, and if I don't find her, I'll move on and you'll be none the poorer."

"You . . . have no idee what that would mean to Martha an' me. I'd thought on goin' out on th' world lookin' fer 'er myself, but I'd have no notion where to start, an' Martha would grieve 'erself to death if'n I left 'er all alone."

"Mr. Harris?"

"Yes?"

"Do you know why your daughter left home?"

"We've tried hard to figger it ourselves. We've picked ourselves to pieces time an' ag'in o'er it, thinkin' mayhap we warn't good 'nough parents an' all. That's nat'ral I guess. But I think she jest got res'less in this lonesome, isolated place, there bein' no other young folks 'er age 'ceptin' Molly, an' Molly workin' as a sody jerk, Martha didn't want Sally gettin' in with 'er an' 'er crowd. An' too, Sally never had no real beau. Makes it real hard on lads an' lasses now'days with no social life to speak of. Th' church kinda went deadlike fer youth. Sally jest kinda *starved* so to speak."

119

"I knowed it was acomin'," Martha added. "I told Henry she was t'home with 'er body but not with 'er heart fer a long spell. She got done with school when she was mere seventeen an' couldn't find a job suited to 'er in these parts. Didn't partic'lar want to teach school er nurse. She's more th' office kind—real smart."

"Er th' housewife kind," chuckled Henry, his fatherly pride showing. "She's a nat'ral cook!"

"That's why we put in th' talkin' box, so in case we got some word from Sally."

"She's never been away from home a single night further than Th' Springs," Henry continued. "So I 'spect wherever she is, she's sorely missin' us. We like to think so, anyways."

"I'm sure she misses you worse than you miss her, Mr. Harris. Most runaways are quite temporary. I'm surprised she hasn't returned before now." ..

"We are, too."

"Unless she met up with someone an' got married."

"Mayhap that's th' reason she run away, Henry . . . to get married." Martha toiled with the new thought.

"Could be."

Married? Jay pushed the thought away. "She didn't leave any kind of message behind?"

"None atall. We went in to town shoppin', an' she said she didn't wanta go. I figger now she had it all planned out. When we got back, she was gone. We knew she had gone away, fer she took her portmanteau an' some clothes with 'er," Martha supplied. "I left 'er a big lunch. Knowin' she had food enough fer a few meals helped my feelin's heaps."

"I'll start my search early in the morning. If you can

spare me, Mr. Harris . . ."

"Let th' cotton go to th' weeds if'n I can have my girl back safe."

"Will you go afoot?" Martha asked.

"Yes. I have a better chance of finding her that way. Would you mind keeping Patches for me?"

"We'll keep Patches ferever if'n you want."

"Tell Molly Rushing you don't know where I am or if I'll ever return."

The Old Lady's Gift

Sally dragged herself from her cot—a poor substitute for a bed—and groped for her clothes, which hung on the back of a nearby chair. Today was Tuesday, the day to clean Mrs. Lindsay's room again. She shuddered. Mrs. Lindsay always said such *frightening* things.

After breakfast, Sally found Mrs. Lindsay waiting for her with her ever-ready-to-talk eagerness.

"Do you ever read the newspaper, girlie?" The old lady laid aside her magnifying glass and squinted at Sally.

"No, ma'am. I seldom have time for reading. But even if I did, I would have no money to purchase one."

"Well, now girlie, that's my one vice—the newspaper. I'd very near do without my Levi Garrett before I'd do without the *Fort Worth Telegram*. Why, that's the best and most informative paper ever printed! Gives all the news in the whole world besides the weather and sports.

Yes, ma'am. I read it from Dan to Beersheba, as my mother used to say, meaning of course from front to back. I never miss a word. Not even the classifieds."

At least the newspaper seemed safer territory for conversation than Indian raids and massacres, so Sally ventured a thin smile.

"I'm sure it's quite educational."

"Yes, indeed! Why, just today there's a piece in here," Mrs. Lindsay thumped the paper dramatically with her forefinger to emphasize her point, "right here it is, about a young girl that was found out on North Belnap Street in an alley behind a nightclub. She was cold-blood murdered . . ."

A tremor ran through Sally's body, reaching even to her fingers that held the feather duster.

"And those classifieds! I get me so amused at the things folks are advertising as lost or to sell or buy or trade with somebody. Why, I wouldn't be surprised to find a notice in there someday for one marm to trade her own children to another marm for six bits to boot." She laughed at her own pitiful humor. "Do you have brothers and sisters, girlie?"

"Yes, ma'am," Sally said quickly, and then to divert the elderly lady's mind, asked in a rush, "Do you have children, Mrs. Lindsay?"

"No, ma'am. Unfortunately, I never was blessed. But I had passels of nieces and nephews, and my house never lacked for the pandemonium brought on by rowdy youngsters."

"I see."

"Now, where was I? What was I saying? Oh, yes, about the lassie that got herself murdered. The paper here says she had long golden hair and blue eyes and was wearing a blue dress. When I read that, I thought first off of you. Now wouldn't you say yourself that the piece kind of describes you? Don't you have a blue dress?"

Sally nodded, her mouth dry.

"One always wonders," the artless woman continued, "what the girl was doing near the saloon anyhow. Of course, she may have been just passing by when someone nabbed her. It isn't safe nowadays for young girls to be away from the protection of home. Why, just about *anything* can happen to them. And the sad thing is, it's usually the wild that know how to survive in the wild while the pure and innocent are the victims of terrible crime. It never seemed quite fair to me."

A nervous half-cough crowded up into Sally's throat. "Uh, the classifieds, Mrs. Lindsay. What . . . do people buy and sell mostly?"

"Anything and everything, girlie! Anything from dirt to gold. Why, one fancy lady wants to sell a ball gown that she's got too fat for. Now, can you imagine that? And for two dollars. What a ridiculous price for a *worn* gown! 'Imported' it says, whatever that means. Then there's a man advertising for a particular kind of saddle.

"Now that don't surprise me any, because Fort Worth is a real cow town just filled to the brim with stockyards and loading pens. And it takes horses to round up cows. You ever been to Fort Worth, girlie?"

Mrs. Lindsay stopped long enough to chuckle, but seemed not to notice that Sally made no answer. "Cowboys are a tough breed, girlie. You ever heard of the Boot Hill cemetery?"

Sally shook her head.

"Well, it's out in Abilene, but cowboys made lots of contributions to that cemetery. A couple of town marshals even got their names engraved on a headstone free up there. I once heard Abilene called a watering place where they served up a dead man for breakfast every morning.

"Anyhow, back to what I was saying. What was I saying? Oh, yes, the cowboys spoiling for trouble and the man looking for a saddle to buy in Fort Worth through the classifieds. I do hope he finds just the right saddle for himself. It's highly important.

"And just listen to this." Mrs. Lindsay situated the magnifying glass, moving it first close to the newsprint and then farther away to make the words larger. " 'Help wanted. Young lady to care for cheerful crippled child. Light housework. Room, board, and excellent salary.' Did you ever think about applying for a job like that, girlie? Have you had any experience with a cripple?"

"Yes, I . . . we . . . our Effie . . ." The words ground to a stop.

"Well, I can tell you one thing, girlie, if you'll take advice from an old widow lady: you're working too hard around this place. You need to look for an easier job. I can see the light fading from your eyes. Before long, you'll be dead *inside,* and that's twice worse than being dead *outside.*"

"I . . . don't believe I would be interested in working in Forth Worth. Do you need your window washed today, Mrs. Lindsay?"

"No, no, don't bother. It's just extra work for your poor tired hands, and I can't see well enough to . . ."

"Then may I say good day?"

"Oh, wait. I didn't finish the story about the pretty

126

girl that was ruthlessly slaughtered. She was about eighteen years old, the newspaper said. But the worst thing is that nobody seems to know who she is or where she is from. Nobody has come to claim her body. The county is burying her today."

Sally inched toward the door.

"Here, girlie, take the newspaper with you. Take it as a gift from me. I'm through reading it, and I'll be getting a new one tomorrow anyhow." Mrs. Lindsay folded the paper carefully and put it into Sally's hand. "Now you will have something to get your mind off your work when you go to your room this evening."

"Thank you, Mrs. Lindsay."

Night had fallen before Sally had a chance to look at the article, and she had to read it by lamplight. *It could have been me.* Her breath came in short sobs. *The night of the storm . . .*

She blew out the lamp and knelt beside the unaccommodating cot. "Oh, thank You, God, for protecting a foolish runaway . . ."

Just as sleep reached for her, she bolted upright in bed, an anguished thought bringing stinging tears to her eyes. What if her parents saw the newspaper story and thought . . . and thought . . . it was *her?* Sarah subscribed to the paper, and Hank read it avidly every morning as he drank his coffee.

She stared out at the starless sky in paralyzed agony. Oh, if daylight would only come! Fears born in the dark often died in the light of day. Hopefully, this one would, too.

In fact, if some of these fears don't die, Sally thought frantically, *I'm afraid I will . . . and then . . . and then . . . a pauper's burial in a nameless grave!*

Chapter Sixteen

Mrs. Gordon's Scissors

"*H*arriet, I'm bringing you my shears, and I want you to cut that long hair off," ordered Mrs. Gordon tersely. "It isn't sanitary around food, and I've had some complaints."

It seemed that a jealous demon had possessed the boarding house proprietress, and with the continual references to Sally's beauty and good cooking, Mrs. Gordon set her head to change Sally—to destroy her physical beauty and make the girl inferior to herself in every way. A lying demon must have come along with his counterpart, for there had never been a derogatory remark from any of the boarders about Sally's long, well-kept hair.

"Oh, I'll always keep my hair up and out of the way when I cook or serve, Mrs. Gordon," promised Sally quickly, alarm shadowing her delicate features. "I've tried to see that it is neat and clean . . ."

"Up isn't good enough. I want it *off.* And *short."*

Sally's cheeks blazed. "I . . . can't cut my hair, Mrs. Gordon. I was my father's tithe baby, and he dedicated me to God . . ."

"God could care less what becomes of that mop of yellow hair, Harriet. But I could. So you'll either obey me or be without a job and homeless again. And bear in mind that the other rooming houses are full up and don't need a slothful cook!" She strutted from the room, her back arched angrily.

Now what do I do, God? she prayed in her bleeding heart. *I'm learning submission . . . but must I take it this far? I could never return to Papa's house with bobbed hair!*

No answer came booming from the sky, so Sally tried to dismiss the incident as one of Mrs. Gordon's idle threats and go on about her work just as before. However, her countenance lacked its usual glow of cheer.

At breakfast, Sally discovered that Mrs. Gordon had "forgotten" to order maple syrup for her famous flapjacks, so she hurriedly made her own vanilla version and served it piping hot. The raves intensified, much to Mrs. Gordon's chagrin.

Mr. Cotterby, Mrs. Gordon's favorite boarder (because he tipped) chose this particular day to put in his appearance. Mrs. Gordon hid her agitation well; she could ill afford to lose this special, extra-revenue customer.

"Be sure to give special attend to Mr. Cotterby," she warned Sally. "And I see that you haven't shorn your hair yet." She glared at Sally, her words sharpening to a point. "I'll be up to your room to do it myself tonight when you finish your chores."

"I see that my special cook is back," Mr. Cotterby

said when Sally delivered his lunch tray. She smiled abstractedly, finding small talk too much effort today.

But Mr. Cotterby was a perceptive man. When she returned to pick up the littered tray, he was waiting, holding his ten-cent tip in his hand. "Do you get the tip or does the landlady?"

"She does."

"Who cooks the food?"

"I do, sir."

"Who dishes it up?"

"I do, sir."

"Who cleans up the dishes?"

"I do, sir."

"Who deserves the tip, then?"

Sally gave him a watered-down smile. "She does, sir."

"Come back when you're finished in the kitchen, and I'll give you the dime."

"Oh, I couldn't do that, sir. I'd get fired!"

"Then bring me up some hot coffee after dinner this evening."

"Yes, sir."

Mrs. Gordon drove Sally especially hard that day. No matter what she did, it failed to please the unreasonable woman. More than once, Sally paused to pray for grace.

When at last the day's work was finished, Mrs. Gordon took Sally by the arm roughly. "We'll go take care of that hair now, Harriet."

"I've one more thing to do before I can retire, Mrs. Gordon."

"What's that?"

"Mr. Cotterby asked for a cup of hot coffee when I had completed my other obligations. If I may be excused to take it to him . . ."

131

"Did Mr. Cotterby put a tip on the tray today?" Mrs. Gordon looked at Sally shrewdly, as if she would look into her soul and find the stolen money hidden there.

"No, ma'am. Perhaps he'll give it to me when I serve him his coffee."

"I can't understand why his tipping has lagged. It's likely something foolish you have said or done to offend him. That's what I get for taking in a homeless waif off the streets that I know nothing about—to take my business to ruination."

Sally felt that her soul shriveled before the biting words.

"But go and take Mr. Cotterby his coffee. And, for this once, be *mannerly*. I'll be in your room waiting with the shears when you return."

Eyes smarting with unshed tears, Sally hurried to the kitchen to make Mr. Cotterby a cup of fresh coffee, arranging it on a serving plate with a white napkin, cream, and sugar. She added a fruit tart left from dinner.

Mr. Cotterby pulled up a chair for Sally. "Please sit down, Miss Harriet."

Sally dropped miserably into the offered chair.

"You're the best little waitress I've ever met."

"Thank you."

"I need to ask a few questions."

"Yes, sir."

"You'll be truthful with me, won't you?"

"I wouldn't willfully lie to you, sir."

"What is your education?"

"I was graduated from a small community academy a year ago May."

"Have you your diploma with you?"

"No, sir."

"From what school did you earn your cap?"

"Brazos Point Community School."

"Would you be willing to sign a release for me to write for your scholastic records?"

"Yes, sir."

"Are you happy working here?"

"No, sir."

"How much does Mrs. Gordon pay you?"

"Just my room and board."

"No money?"

"None, sir."

Mr. Cotterby's facial muscles tightened, causing his words to come out huskily. "Is Mrs. Gordon putting pressure on you?"

"Yes, sir."

"In what way?"

"She's waiting in my room with the shears to cut my hair and make it very short."

"To do *what?*"

"Cut all my hair off."

"Do you want your hair cut short?"

"Oh, no, sir!"

"Well, of all the gall!"

"Please, sir, don't say anything to Mrs. Gordon about our conversation. She already feels that I am endangering her business . . ."

"Endangering her business? In what way?"

"I wouldn't know, sir."

"Let me inform you, Miss Harriet, that you are *bringing* the old lady business with your superb cooking. If you hadn't come along just when you did, I wouldn't still be patronizing this place. The food had become indigestible!"

"If you'll excuse me, Mr. Cotterby . . ."

"No, wait, Miss Harriet. Would you be interested in another job?"

"Oh, that would be quite impossible, sir!"

"Why so?"

"I haven't been out of this house but once since I came here more than a month ago. I haven't time . . . and if I took another job, I'd have no place to stay. Mrs. Gordon would put me out on the street."

"So you feel you are caught in a vicious carousel?"

"I'm afraid so, sir. I'm . . . praying for a way out. But I've so much to learn. Perhaps God is molding me in submission."

"I doubt that God has anything to do with it," spat the telephone tycoon, touched by Sally's humility. "It sounds more like the devil to me."

Sally moved toward the door, fearful lest Mrs. Gordon would come searching for her.

"Miss Harriet, I'll help you if you'll let me."

Sally grew apprehensive. "I couldn't take money . . ."

"I'm not offering charity. I'm looking for four high school graduates to work in the new telephone exchange here. The wages are excellent for a woman, and we train. You could have your choice of being a local or a long distance operator. The hours and pay are the same."

Sally's expression lighted, then darkened again. "But, I couldn't . . ."

"Why?"

"I'd have no place to stay until I received my first paycheck."

"I've worked ahead of you. My sister lives across the

134

river in Pleasant Valley. She's a widow with no children yet at home. She would be happy to provide you a nice bedroom, and you could share meals with her. It would relieve her loneliness to have a girl like you around—and she wouldn't chase you with the scissors." Mischief danced in Mr. Cotterby's blue eyes.

"She only lives a few blocks from the office where you would be working. Now you probably wonder why I don't live with her instead of in this grimy boarding house. The fact is, we both felt that my presence there might incite gossip by those who wouldn't know we were related. Sis is very proper. She's not only conscientious, but she is a wonderful Christian."

Mr. Cotterby's proposal seemed a fantasy; Sally waited to awaken and find the words untrue, crumbling like sand castles.

"Oh, I could pay her back out of my very first paycheck!"

"You can settle that with Sis, but I'm sure she won't hear to it. The pleasure will be all hers to have a companion. When can you start to work for our company?"

The tension bled away. Sally smiled a beautiful, happy smile. "Right now."

"There's only one requirement my sister will have, and I'll concur with her on that."

The tension crept back into Sally's sad, worn eyes. "What is that, sir?"

"She'll want you to keep your long hair. She's old-fashioned and quite adverse to the modern girls with their mannish bobs."

"I'd be only too glad . . ." Sally shuddered. "But Mrs. Gordon is twice my size and is waiting. I'm afraid I can't stop her."

"I'd best go with you and explain. If Mrs. Gordon gives me any hassle, I'll threaten to find lodging elsewhere when I'm working in this area. With Mrs. Gordon, money talks."

Mrs. Gordon sat snapping the scissors open and shut, her thick lips moving omniously. She jerked around angrily when Sally and Mr. Cotterby entered the room. "What has the clumsy girl done now, Mr. Cotterby?" she scorned. "Whatever it is, I'll do my best to make amends. You understand, of course, that I was already thinking of firing her."

"Please put down those dangerous scissors, Mrs. Gordon," the calm man suggested. "I fear you are going to put your eyes out if you don't stop waving them around in the atmosphere like that."

Mrs. Gordon, embarrassed, dropped the swinging scissors into her lap.

"What had you planned to do with the scissors, ma'am?"

"Well, I was measuring the room for some curtains, and . . ."

"And what else?"

There was an awkward silence. "I thought while I was in here . . . uh . . . that I'd just trim Harriet's hair from about her face a bit and smooth those frazzled ends. Hair is unsanitary about food you know and . . ."

"It won't be at all necessary for you to groom Miss Harriet's hair, Mrs. Gordon," Mr. Cotterby told her with authority that only a man of his station could wield, "because she won't be working with food after tonight. I've just hired her on as a long distance telephone operator . . ."

"Oh, but I couldn't let her go, of course, Mr. Cotterby. She's the best employee I've ever had, and I depend on her to do my cooking and yours, you know. Besides, I can't let her stay on here for free until . . . uh, until she gets paid by your company."

"That's all arranged for, Mrs. Gordon. A relative of mine has a lovely furnished bedroom just waiting for Miss Harriet. If you don't mind, I'll take her to her new quarters tonight."

He turned to Sally. "Could you gather your clothing while I wait? I wish to get back here as early as possible and get a good night's rest. I have a very important meeting in the morning."

Mrs. Gordon still tried to object. "I'll be available to help her gather her belongings, Mr. Cotterby," she said cagily. "You can step into the sitting room and wait there for her."

"No, I'll just wait here and take her baggage out for her if you don't mind."

So Mrs. Gordon had no chance to speak to Sally alone. Nor did she even mention the four-bit deposit that she had promised to return to Sally if she "checked out properly."

Chapter Seventeen

Troubles for Jay

"*M*ay I speak to Mr. Walls, please?" Molly's lips, red with excess lipstick, parted in a sly, artificial smile.

"I'm sorry, Molly," Martha returned her best fabricated politeness. "Mr. Walls ain't here."

Molly gasped. "But he'll *have* to come back, Mrs. Harris. We are planning to be married soon."

"I guess'n you can't marry someun what ain't even here."

"You have no idea where he went?"

"Absolutely none."

Patches pulled himself from beneath the porch, stretched and yawned.

"You are lying to me, Mrs. Harris! There's Jay's spotted dog!"

"He give us th' animal if'n he never gits back."

Molly looked at Martha scornfully, tiny points of light

glinting in her violet eyes. "You've always hated me, Martha Harris. You got it in for me when your son . . . loved me. You are behind this . . . this . . . driving of my fiance away so he would be out of my reach! But I'll get him yet, you'll see!"

The scorching words were meant to wither Martha but, in fact, they did not.

"Think what you please, Miss Molly. Th' young man made 'is own decision to leave with us'ns just beggin' fer 'im to stay with us."

"I don't believe you! Let me talk to Mr. Harris! Mr. Harris will tell me the truth. Everyone knows him to be *honest.*"

When Henry substantiated Martha's story, Molly strutted off haughtily, stumbling on a small stone and scarcely regaining her footing in time to avert a headlong plunge.

Molly was not at church Sunday morning; Myrt said the girl took herself back to The Springs in a fit of mad. The church organist was visibly upset. Her cold stare bode no friendliness when the Harrises took their bench.

The parson had not expected Martha and Henry to be in attendance that morning. Word had sizzled through the telephone lines that Sally Harris had been ignominiously murdered in "the big city." The news reached his ears only hours prior to the service.

Through a twisted grapevine of conflicting reports it came. "I heared Sarah reportin' it to her mother with mine own ears," one good sister persisted.

"Yes, an' th' way I got it, they ain't never located th' murderer, either," told another importantly.

"They's a big mystery 'bout th' whole story . . . Poor

Brother and Sister Harris. To have sech a black blotch attached to their good fam'ly record . . ."

So their presence at church, with normal and un-abashed greetings, brought skeptical whispers of something "in hiding."

Myrt initiated her personal campaign to determine where Jay was and why he left; a man of this quality must not escape her careless granddaughter. She called on Brother Stevens that very afternoon. "Pastor Stevens, do you know anything about Jay Walls?"

"I made his acquaintance . . ."

"Tell me all you know."

"Well, Sister Myrt, I . . ."

"I don't want no hum-hawin', Pastor."

"He's from the northwest edge of our state . . ."

"But I want to know . . ."

"He's a Christian, though a very blinded one."

"That's not what I'm interested in, Brother Stevens. *Where* did Jay go?"

"Is he gone?"

"Yes. Leastwise Martha Harris says he is."

"Why, I wouldn't have a notion, Sister Myrt. I didn't even know he had left . . ."

"And here with him supposed to marry my Molly just any day now!"

"I'd just count it a blessing, Sister Myrt. The Bible says all things work together for the best . . ."

"Jay was by far the gentlemanest young man Molly ever set her heart on."

"You might ask Brother Henry . . ."

"Molly went to the Harrises and didn't get no satisfaction a tall. But I intend on gettin' to th' *bottom* o' this

141

matter. If'n they've hid him, they'll pay." She waddled off in a huff.

The parson shook his weary head; trouble was brewing, and how he detested it!

Myrt puffed her way to Martha's front door. "Why, come in, Myrt!" Martha greeted cheerfully, removing her apron and making a place for Myrt to sit.

"I come to talk about Jay Walls."

"Why, certainly . . .'"

"I didn't expect a man with such high ideals to walk out on a promise he made to my granddaughter."

"He went away on urgent business, Myrt."

"Jest what sort o' business is that, Martha?"

"Some personal business I'm not free to discuss."

"Then he'll be back soon?"

"I don't know."

"He didn't say when he'd return?"

"No, he didn't. He said he might not never be back, an' if'n he warn't ever back, fer us'ns to take good keer o' his dog. He was fond o' that dog. Th' animal's a'ready missin' 'is master, poor mutt. But 'twas th' most touchin' thing, Myrt. He went out an' had a good long talk with that dog afore he left that mornin' an' told 'im to be content with me an' Henry an' that we'd take precious good keer o' him. Why, that dog's as smart as a human bein'. He knowed what Jay was sayin'. Why, that dog can might near talk! I always wanted a dog 'round th' place . . ."

Myrt tired of the sidetracking. "You don't even know which *direction* Jay went?"

"Took off t'ward th' river, Henry said."

"That don't tell me nuthin'."

"Me neither," Martha said nonchalantly.

"Did he leave any word fer my Molly?"

"He shore did. He said tell her he might not be returnin'."

Myrt studied the unperturbed Martha. The community buzzed with news of Sally's death, and yet Martha acted as though she had not been informed of the tragedy. An investigation was in order.

"Have you any news from Sally, Martha?" she asked abruptly, focusing her narrow eyes on Martha's face to detect any change of expression.

"No, but I expect she's doin' just fine, er she'd let us know."

"Then . . . it was only a rumor that Sally . . ."

Martha finished the sentence for her. "Was killed? Yes, 'twas someone jest jumpin' to conclusions, thank th' Lord. Sally ain't in Fort Worth . . . she ain't never been there."

Myrt, more confused than ever, left brooding, convinced that Martha knew Jay's whereabouts and his destination. "Somethin's fishy," she muttered aloud. "Somebody's lyin', an' Martha Harris knows somethin' she ain't tellin'."

Miles away, Jay followed the winding waterway, checking every cove and nook for the telltale boat. At night he made himself a bed of leaves, using his knapsack for a pillow. He stretched the food Martha sent, stopping at hamlets on the river to buy cheese, crackers, and raisins now and then. He found that his mission brought him immeasurable happiness. Was it that he wanted to see the lovely girl once again, or was it merely to bring peace to the waiting parents to whom he owed much?

In a conversational manner, he inquired of those he

met along the way if they had seen Sally. Past the railroad
bridge where he first spotted her, his search intensified.
Two burly men of hard countenance, bronzed dark by
many shirtless hours in the baking sun, rolled barrels from
a dock. As Jay approached, they sat down to mop sweat
from their faces. The older of them, his handlebar
moustache constantly atwitch, wore a hat drawn low.

"Going somewhere or just joy walking?" one of the
brutes yelled caustically.

"Want my job?" the other tauted.

"How's the pay?" Jay returned jovially.

"Lousy."

Jay sat down on the wharf beside them. "I'm looking for a friend," he said.

"Ain't nobody but us two and the boss works here,
mister," spoke up the hatted man. "Either of us the friend
you're looking for?"

"You're not the right . . . gender."

The younger man slapped the other's knee. "Did you
hear that insult, Sarge?"

"If it's a lady he's looking for, let's help him find her!"
A wicked snicker passed between them. Their effrontery
sickened Jay's heart, and he wished he had never stopped.

"Tell us about her, pardner. What's her looks?"

Jay hesitated, wanting to protect her purity and innocence from these boorish characters.

"Well, speak up!"

"She's . . . lovely. She has golden hair, sky blue eyes,
and . . ."

"Monroe! That's our mermaid he's talking about! Did
she come down the river in a little flat-bottomed boat,
mister?"

Jay bolted to attention. "Yes, she did. When did you see her?"

"Oh, it must have been several weeks ago now since we seen her passing this way. She was tied up to a tree and asleep when we first found her. While we was arguing which one of us she belonged to, she woke up and got scared and got away from both of us. Tough luck." He picked a splinter from a rough board and rolled it in his teeth.

"I was for swimming out and fetching her back, but we was almost late for work already."

"We should have forgot the work. There's always work, but Goldilockses are mighty scarce."

"Yep, and she passed right here after we got to work."

"But, Sarge, we seen her since that, remember?"

"Oh, yes, yes. We was downriver at that place called . . ."

"Fort Fisher."

"That's it. Old Indian place."

"When was that?" Jay inquired diligently.

"About a week ago. Right after last paycheck. We went in to have a little . . ."

Sarge put his filthy hand across his crony's mouth. "Don't say it, Monroe. This sonny looks too lily-white and churchy to dirty his ears with the places we hang out."

"Anyhow, we were in this naughty joint. Sarge was filled up to the brim. A big storm came up, and the girl snuck in the entryway for protection from the weather. Sarge, all stewed, scared the poor mermaid and she ran away."

Sarge snickered. "But what a blowout we had with

145

the bag of duds she left behind. Ole Monroe there did a modeling job for us with her perty blue dress. And man, does he look funny in ruffles and lace." At the hilarious memory, the man doubled in sensuous laughter.

Jay's anger flared. It cost him a tongue-biting to remain silent.

"She disappeared into the flood—and we hoped she'd come back to fetch her sack and dance for us, but she never did."

"It was about midnight. I don't know where she was headed for, but she's probably drowned or dead of pneumonia by now."

Jay shrank from the bitter word *pneumonia*. How it haunted him!

He nodded his head toward the men and started away, disheartened and discouraged.

"And if you find her, boy," one of the rascals called after him, "tell her she'll find her clothes behind the counter of Butch's Bar, smelling a little boozy." When he lifted his shaggy hat in a farewell salute, Jay saw the coarse scar at his hairline.

Jay clenched his fists and ran, afraid of what he would do if he heard more.

Chapter Eighteen

Follow Up

*E*ven the garish, outdated hat did little to hide Mrs. Gordon's antagonistic spirit as she stood at Mrs. Mason's front door viciously clanging the door knocker. She was determined to find "Harriet."

Her leaving the boarding house, even for an hour, caused suspicious whispers in the dusky sitting room. "Never seen Sister Gordon so spruced up," a thin man's voice rankled behind his coarse laugh. "And I've been here better than a year. Mayhap she's going out sparking and we'll get us another proprietor. Now, wouldn't that be grand?"

"Say, what happened to the little pretty that did the fluffy biscuits?" asked his cohort. "I thought we'd done died and gone to heaven when I put my old toothless mouth on those softies! I couldn't even *gum* those rocks Old Lady Gordon served up for breakfast this morning.

And to think she has the unmitigated gall to even *call* them biscuits! What's this world coming to?"

"I heard she fired our pretty cook."

"Fired her? The pretty probably up and walked out on the old grouch. I would have. You know, squire, as long as that little missy was here, I never heard that old soul speak a single kind word to her. And the child worked like a railroad hand from daylight until dark."

Gracie Lindsay, sitting in a faded horsehair chair nearby and reading her newspaper with the old faithful magnifying glass, spoke up. "I wasn't born yesterday, gentlemen. And my eyesight may be poorly, but my ears haven't lost none of their capacity. And being as my room is close on to where the lassie stayed, I *heard* what happened to the girlie."

"Why, of course, Mrs. Lindsay. And would you care to enlighten us as to what happened to our dear biscuit maker?" the thin man asked, holding his curiosity with loose rein and ready spur.

"You'll have to let me start at the beginning . . ."

"Take all the time you need," the toothless man grinned and pushed back in his chair, his hands locked behind a head of thinning gray hair.

"Oh, the night the girlie left, I was sitting in my room just athinking, What if the Indians raid again tonight like they did right here long ago? It's been almost fifty years . . ."

"Please don't start *that* far back, Mrs. Lindsay."

Mildly annoyed at the interruption so early in her story, Mrs. Lindsay folded her hands patiently.

"But do go on," goaded the second.

"As I was saying . . . what was I saying? Oh, yes. I

heard a clicking noise coming from the girlie's room, and I knew for a fact that the girlie was not in her room yet. So I tippytoed quietly down the hall to have a look. And guess what I found?"

"We couldn't venture a guess. Do tell us, Mrs. Lindsay!"

"There sat Mrs. Gordon in the girlie's room with her scissors, just a-snapping away at the air like a mad woman! She had a wild look in her eyes and her lips were moving, but she wasn't saying a word. It just gave me the *creeps*. I thought she had *snapped*. You know, people do that sometimes. Their mind just up and leaves. Now take my Aunt Prunilla Gertrude. She was just going along fine, and one day her husband, Bocephus, found her sitting in the flower bed trying to feed the daisies her cornmeal mush with a spoon and . . ."

"Ahem . . . Mrs. Lindsay . . ."

"As I was saying . . . what was I saying? Oh, yes. About those scissors. I was afraid if I spoke up and startled her, she might charge at me, using those sharp scissors for a weapon. You never know what addled people will do, you know. Now my Aunt Prunilla . . ."

She caught the scant man's frown.

"Anyway, I tippytoed back to my room, planning to stop the girlie on her way to her room, for fear that Mrs. Gordon would harm her."

"Did you stop her?"

"No, sir, I didn't. By and by here comes the girlie down the hall, but she wasn't by her lonesome self. That big telephone man—what's his name?"

"Cotterby?"

"That's the name. You know, I used to know a Cotterby back in '73. I wonder if there would be any chance of relation there. Of course, that was before telephones were brought to these parts. Aren't those talking machines the limit, though? Once I tried to talk on one and I . . ."

"Mrs. Lindsay . . ."

"Oh, yes. As I was saying. Now what *was* I saying?" The elderly lady had gone completely blank.

"The girl and Mr. Cotterby," prompted her listener.

"Yes, yes. That's it. Mr. Cotterby and the girlie were going toward the girlie's room together."

"You don't say?"

"I do say. And you needn't let your evil mind think there was any hanky-panky going on betwixt the two, because there wasn't!" she flared indignantly.

"Of course not, Mrs. Lindsay," placated the old man quickly. "So?"

"The girlie apparently knew—though I never figured out how—that Mrs. Gordon was in the room, and she took Mr. Cotterby for protection."

"Quite naturally."

"Now like I said . . . what did I say? Oh, yes. My eyes may be bad, but my ears aren't. So I heard every word that was said."

"Yes?"

"Mr. Cotterby asked Mrs. Gordon to please quit waving the scissors about in the air. He said he feared that she would put her eyes out with them. You know that has happened. Now take for instance my nephew's youngest son, Thorndale Junior. He was playing with his mother's sewing shears when she wasn't looking and . . ."

"Please, Mrs. Lindsay . . ."

"And as I was saying . . . what was I saying? Oh . . . Mr. Cotterby. Then he asked Mrs. Gordon what she was doing in the girlie's room with the scissors anyhow."

"And Mrs. Gordon said . . . ?"

"Give me time! Give me time! She said she was measuring the room for curtains."

"Measuring with scissors? Now I always thought you measured with a rule, didn't you, squire?"

Mrs. Lindsay held the man with her watery eyes. "I'll thank you not to interrupt, sir."

"Pardon, madam."

"Somehow Mr. Cotterby didn't quite believe her, I guess. He asked what *else* she had in mind with those scissors . . ."

"She didn't plan to actually harm the child, did she?"

"Now, sir, if you want *me* to tell . . ."

"Oh, *begging* pardon, madam. Go right ahead."

"After a bit of awkward silence, Mrs. Gordon said that she planned to cut the girlie's hair off with the scissors. She said long hair was messy about food and that long hair and food didn't mix."

Her listeners gasped but remained obediently silent.

"Then in a real official voice, Mr. Cotterby told Mrs. Gordon that it wouldn't be necessary for her to give the girlie a haircut because thereafter the girlie would be working for his telephone company instead of here at the boarding house—and long, beautiful hair wouldn't be a drawback at the telephone place."

"So that's what happened to our biscuit maker."

"Yes, that's what. And you should have heard the squawk Mrs. Gordon put up. She got nicety-nicety and said she couldn't let the girlie go because she was the best cook anywhere and to let her go would mean she'd lose business. But that didn't work either. Then she tried every way in the world to talk Mr. Cotterby into waiting here in the lobby while she 'helped' the girlie gather her belongings. She had her sly motives, of course. But Mr. Cotterby wouldn't leave. He said he'd stay and help tote the baggage. He's a sharp cookie, that Mr. Cotterby. And him a bachelor! Why, if I was just a little younger . . .''

"I guess I kept hoping our little pretty was just on a wee vacation and would be back, and I'd get to taste one more of those angel biscuits before I moved on." The remorseful words came from the pink-gummed man.

"And Mrs. Gordon lost another boarder just today," Mrs. Lindsay supplied with her all-knowing nod. "When she put on that ridiculous hat and went out this morning, I said to myself, said I, 'Gracie, your old landlady has taken herself in search of that girlie. Because she knows if she *don't* get her back, this boarding house is going to look like a ghost town.' The biscuits are like coffee: if you haven't ever tasted coffee, you might be satisfied with milk, but once you've tasted coffee, you're never satisfied . . ."

"I believe I'll go to my room, squire."

"And as I was saying . . . what was I saying? Oh, yes. Mr. Cotterby told Mrs. Gordon that the girlie would be staying with a relative of his. I dare say she snooped around until she found that relative's address. She's probably clapping the knocker right now!"

Meanwhile, across the river, Seth Cotterby's sister heard the heavy knocking and hurried to the front door. It took concerted effort not to stare at the puffy-faced apparition that stood there.

"I'm looking for a Miss Harriet," Mrs. Gordon barked.

"Miss Harriet is resting and I prefer not to disturb her," Mrs. Mason smiled, but even the smile suggested polite dismissal.

"I'm Gordon, the boarding house owner across the river. I've come to take Miss Harriet back to her job. Your brother carted her off quite . . . abruptly. I'm losing customers since she left. I can't do all the work myself, and the tenants are complaining about my cooking."

"I'm sorry. Miss Harriet will not be available for your employ."

"But I'll . . . I'll even *pay* her!"

"You mean you didn't pay her while she worked for you?"

"Yes. No. I mean, this time I'll pay her in *money.*"

"Her beautiful golden hair is worth more than all the money in the state of Texas, Mrs. Gordon. Good day."

Mrs. Gordon found herself staring at the wooden door that had just closed unceremoniously in her face.

Chapter Nineteen

Identity Crisis

"*H*ave we ever had a graduate from our community school by the name of Sal Harriet?" Pastor Stevens, still acting chairman of the school board after his temporary appointment of many years past, asked his wife.

"Never heard the name."

"Who would have the register?"

"It would be at the school, I suppose. Why?"

"We have a request for a record of graduation for someone by that name. It's from the telephone company in Waco."

"What year did the person graduate? Must have been back past our time."

"It says last year."

"There must have been a mistake, dear. The document was evidently sent to the wrong address. Write and tell them they have the wrong school."

155

"Are you certain that there wasn't anyone by that name even for a piece of the term?"

"I'm sure. There was only four diplomas given last year. They were Molly Rushing, Winifred Jamison, and Sally Harris from here and Richard Caldwell from over at Eulogy."

"I'll write this Mr. Cotterby and tell him we've never graduated anyone last-named Harriet."

Pastor Stevens posted the letter and forgot the incident, while in the town where the request for the transcript originated, Sally awoke, still marveling at her sudden "new world."

She wiggled her toes under the lavender-scented sheets, her emotions wobbling from tears to laughter. *As soon as I get my first pay, I'll buy a stamp and post Mama and Papa a long letter so they won't worry.*

Scents of summer climbers wafted through the low window on the refreshing breeze. Sally could see them blooming in ruby red clusters on the picket fence. Lacy white curtains framed the perfect picture. What a contrast to the poor accommodations of the rooming house! Here she even had a clothespress in which to hang her dresses. Clean baseboards, flowered wallpaper, and a soft feather bed swept her worlds away from the "prison" across the river.

And a day off? The luxury of an hour of repose past daylight surpassed all other extravagances. Mrs. Mason insisted on it, fussing over Sally's sunken eyes that were undergirded by dark half-moon shadows.

Sally could hear Mrs. Mason in the kitchen singing as she flitted about her work, reminding one of a busy hummingbird. Next to her own mother, Sally loved Seth

Cotterby's sister better than any woman she had ever met. Almost she had told her "everything," but she decided to wait until her period of job training ended and her job was secure.

Her month of "schooling" before her first check had not dragged as badly as she feared it would. With two weeks behind her, there were two to go. Although she enjoyed her work, it would please her to take the initial money she earned and rush home to the arms of her beloved parents, but propriety would never let her do that. Mr. Cotterby did not train her to quit after one month; that would be an injustice on her part, showing ingratitude. She contemplated asking him someday how long it would take to "fulfill her week" as Jacob had done in Bible days. She hoped it wasn't seven years. Even so, perhaps she could go to Brazos Point by rail on weekends and holidays to ease the pain of those dear, lonely hearts.

Thoughts of home brought tears; thoughts of how God delivered her from the clutches of Mrs. Gordon and the loathsome boarding house brought thanksgiving.

Mrs. Mason tiptoed in with a cup of tea. Seeing Sally awake, she asked, "How did you rest, Sal?"

"Just wonderful, thank you."

"One should never face the new day without a cup of famous Cotterby tea."

"I wouldn't think of trying!"

Placing the china cup and saucer on the bedside table, Mrs. Mason sat down on the quiltbox nearby. "Seth stopped by while I was out weeding the petunias early this morning," she said amiably. "He left a message for you."

"Mr. Cotterby left me a message?"

"Yes, and spent the rest of the time bragging on your abilities."

"Oh."

"He told me you were learning so fast that he might be able to get you a promotion right away. He said he figured that you would want to advance with the company as fast as you were able, since you had been left homeless and had the total responsibility of your living to earn in the future."

Sally looked away. "I appreciate . . . Mr. Cotterby's interest."

"I knew I couldn't keep you. Good things like you just don't last . . ."

Sally laughed, but her voice came shallow. "I don't suppose I'll be going anywhere . . . for a while anyhow."

"Seth said the higher paying job would probably be down at the state capital."

"Austin?"

"Yes."

"How . . . far away is that?"

"At least a hundred miles."

"Oh, I don't . . ." Sally bit off her words. *Farther from home? If I leave the river, I might never find my way back to Mama.*

"I know it would be frightening in a way," soothed Mrs. Mason, seeing Sally's distress. "And you are so young to be alone in a great city. That's what I told Seth. How old are you, Sal?"

"Half between eighteen and nineteen."

"That's a tender age to be orphaned."

Sally averted her eyes from Mrs. Mason's sympathetic gaze, looking into her teacup uncomfortably. Sensing the discomfort the conversation caused, Mrs. Mason hastened on. "Seth says you have very good rapport with the other employees."

"I . . . hope so."

"He said the only problem he has had—and it's minor—is obtaining your school records. He sent for your records without your signature, but felt that would be insignificant."

"I . . . don't understand. Only four of us graduated last year . . ."

"That's what the return letter said. Seth let me read it. It was from a Mr. Stevens . . ."

"Yes. He should be able to verify my graduation."

"But your name wasn't on the graduation list."

"It wasn't?"

"No. He said they had no knowledge of a Miss Sal Harriet."

Flames of shame began in Sally's chest, sending a searing heat up her throat and splashing thick burning color across her face. Her lie about her name had caught up with her. "Be sure your sin will find you out," was the first Scripture verse Martha had taught her. Now events had proved its accuracy.

Of course there was no Sal Harriet!

"I'm . . . sorry," muttered Sally. "Did . . . he . . . Mr. Stevens send the names of the graduates?"

"Yes, but I have forgotten them. I was interested only in yours. I'm sure there's a mistake—please don't be so alarmed, child! Mr. Cotterby will be back to straighten it all out for you. Your job is not in jeopardy."

"Was . . . there a Sally Harris?"

"Let me think. There were two girls and two boys,

I believe. Yes, it seems to me that that was the name of one of the girls."

"The other was Molly?"

"That's it! Sally and Molly. And your name was left off."

Sally straightened her thin shoulders that carried the heavy load of guilt, resolved to straighten her "inner man" as well. With a lump in her throat and blazing cheeks, she whispered her confession. "I am Sally Harris, a runaway and a liar." She could find no pretty way to say it, but the ugly words found their beauty in a casement of repentance and humility.

Mrs. Mason, refusing to heap condemnation on the girl, said simply, "Your actions and motives are not mine to question, child."

"I do have a family . . . a very *lovely* family," Sally exposed, anxious to bare her heart to someone, anyone. "I'm the youngest of ten. Nine are yet alive. I also had a crippled foster sister who saved my life when I was a baby.

"After I finished school last year, I wanted to go to work in town, but there were no job openings that my mother considered 'respectable' for a young lady. Mama is quite old-fashioned . . ."

"I'm sure I would like her," interrupted Mrs. Mason. "And I wouldn't want to be an accomplice to something she would not wish you to do. Do you think, Sally, that your mother would approve of you being a telephone operator?"

"Yes, I believe she would, Mrs. Mason. I don't think you have to worry about that. I . . . think she and Papa would both be proud of me. That would be in the class with a schoolmarm, would it not?"

"I think it would. Go on with your story, Sally. Why did you leave such a good home?"

"I was very foolish, Mrs. Mason. The spirit of the prodigal became mine. I got bored and lonely on the farm. I entertained feelings of rebellion until they became a part of me, and I decided I was old enough and big enough to chart my own destiny . . ."

"Do you still feel that way?"

"Oh, no! I've been a miserable failure! When I saw what a hopeless mess I was in at Mrs. Gordon's boarding house, I gave my life back to God and now *He's* charting my course."

"Do you miss your parents a great deal, Sally?"

Tears sifted through Sally's long, feathered lashes, paused at her nose, and then slid to her chin. "Yes, ma'am. I miss them . . . dreadfully."

"Have you contacted them at all?"

"Not . . . yet. I wrote them a letter, but . . . never mailed it."

"Have you a reason for not letting them know that you are safe?"

Sally could not bring herself to ask for even as small a favor as a postage stamp. "I . . . wasn't able."

"But you will, child?"

"I will, Mrs. Mason . . . before . . . long now."

"You must be very special to God, Sally, or He wouldn't spend so much effort on you," Mrs. Mason said gently. "I can see that He is building something beautiful. He wants our whole heart, but He'll take it in pieces—if He can just have all the pieces."

Sally managed a small, strained smile. "Thank you, Mrs. Mason. I must be special to God, or He wouldn't have sent me to . . . you."

161

Cold Trail

"*W*here did you get that boat, sir?" Jay asked the loose-jointed, hollow-cheeked fellow that docked in the cove. There could only be one boat in the entire universe like it. Jay would have recognized it anywhere, even minus its heart-stopping cargo.

"Bought it off'n one of the shipping workers upstream," the man clipped, his expressionless black eyes roving past Jay to the jutting post where he planned to lash his raft.

"Do you know where he got it?"

The man shrugged noncommittally. "Nope."

"Did you buy it . . . here?"

"It beached here for quite a spell before I bought it."

"What was the name of the man who sold it to you?"

The gangling, low-jawed man dropped his bony hand to his side and stared at Jay coldly. "I don't *know* the man's name. Met him in a bar. Are you trying to accuse me of *stealing* this boat or something, mister?"

Jay flushed. "Oh, no sir! I didn't mean to be . . . rude. I . . . it's just that I've seen the boat before, knew its previous owner, and am looking for . . ."

"A deal is a deal."

"The last time I saw it, it carried . . . a young lady passenger. I'm trying to locate her . . . and I'm reasoning that she'll be somewhere in the area where . . . she sold the boat."

"I dunno about that. I never knew a girl owned it. Boats don't have papers like land, you know. I bought it from a man that has a scar about where his face stops and his hair starts. You might find him some weekend in a place called Butch's Bar. Fort Fisher's the town. He's there most Saturday nights. But I paid him fair and square for this dinghy, though he probably gambled the price of it away before the dawn."

"Thank you, sir."

Jay wound his way through the river port's streets, following much the same path that Sally had taken. The sight of the familiar craft goaded him on; it was the very clue he had hoped to find. His bloodshot eyes searched everywhere for her face, his head throbbing from the sleeplessness of the past three days.

The ill-famed bar, its wretched doors barred and bolted, stood deceptively quiet. Its daytime facade awaited the blackness of night to begin the hours of rollick. His eyes found the portico where Sally had sought shelter from the elements, where the villains had taunted her when they had frightened her in their drunken debauchery. He had gone a full block before his fists relaxed, releasing the tight white knuckles that were weary with restraint.

He wandered on. His body seemed to be going nowhere in mad circles while his mind begged for respite. At length, fatigue drove him to seek a place to sleep, though he begrudged the wasted time spent on his "human weaknesses." He checked in at the City Hotel, a poor, threadbare excuse for a sleeping facility.

Pigeons skittered about on a corregated tin roof nearby. Crickets chirped in the cracks of the dirty floor. Smoke from factories fogged screenless windows. The orchestra of distraction banished any thought of peaceful rest. But Jay "slept piecemeal," as his aged grandmother would have said.

Although he had scant hopes of learning anything of Sally in this sin-filled area, he inquired of a tobacco-stained patron of the hotel as he checked out. He was surprised when the watery eyes of the seedy dwelling's resident registered ready cognizance.

"A girl with gold-spun hair-like, you say, laddie? Wal, yeah, I seen one such sweetheart-like girl pass here back along the first of the season-like . . ."

"Which way did she go from here, sir?"

"She went thataway." The great-nosed man jerked his begrimed thumb toward the railway station. "Thought there for a minute she was gonna turn in here-like, but she just kind of hesitated-like then shifted her bag to the other arm-like and walked on right quick-like . . ."

"She saw you," interjected a lazing listener. "You're bad for business."

"I watched her as far as I could see down the street-like . . ."

Jay thanked him and hurried away, catching his foot on a loose board in front of the sagging door. *The railroad station! What if Sally had boarded the train here for an unknown destination?* The suffocating thought reached out to choke him. *Would the ticket agent remember her . . . or what train she took?*

He ran, blinded by a reckless abandon, to the railway station and found the bespectacled clerk busy at the monotonously clicking telegraph. When Jay inquired about Sally, the agent clattered out the answers to his questions as methodically as the insensitive machine still spitting out its printed information.

From the dialogue, Jay learned that a girl fitting Sally's description came into the station with her baggage "six or eight weeks ago, maybe longer." She asked for a quote on railway fares, then took her leave without purchasing a ticket and had not returned. *In that event, she's here somewhere,* Jay told himself. *And I won't give up until I find her.*

All recommendations for lodging dovetailed for Mrs. Gordon's boarding house. Gregarious, longtime residents said her rooms were cleaner and cooler, and her rates included meals and coffee anytime. The other rooming places were "flophouses," Jay was told.

"Heard say old lady Gordon had the best cook on the continent there for a while," one old-timer reported. "Folks were standing in line to get a room just to taste the biscuits and gravy. But some say she ain't been there of late, and the food is greasy-spoon again like it used to be, and folks is beginning to move out. Maybe there'll be a vacancy now."

"She houses the uppity when they come to town on

business," said another. "The big telephone man stays there. You here on business or permanent?"

"On business."

"Well, I wouldn't advise you to stay on permanent. You look tame. We're not tame people around here," the informer suppressed a string of oaths. "River towns come by wickedness honest."

Jay secured a room at Mrs. Gordon's, reflecting that if this seamy inn represented the finest of lodging in town, he should loath seeing the lesser accommodations—though it was a cut above the City Hotel. Fat Mrs. Gordon herself showed him to his room, reciting the rules in a dull, even monotone. "You married or single?" she threw in.

"Single."

"Don't want no coming in at all hours of the night in my establishment," she barked. "If you try it, you'll find yourself locked out."

Jay paid his deposit, listing his old address on the name card. Then he unpacked his duffle bag, arranging its contents on the rickety dressing table.

He let his eyes explore the skeletal room for which he paid dearly. The warped mirror distorted his reflection, its crack breaking his forehead into two parts. The top set of bleary eyes peered from near his well-oiled hair while the lower set came close to his nose. The hideous double made Jay smile, but the glass contorted it to a grimace.

A bit of ribbon caught on the clothes hook behind the door commanded his attention. Its tiny splash of color, feebly struggling to cheer up the drab room, lifted Jay's spirits. Obviously a girl had once occupied the room. The sweet, clean smell of her clothing still hung heavy in the room like a perfume, overpowering less pleasant odors. For one thrilling moment, his heart jumped with an exhilarating thought. *Could the former occupant have been Sally?* Then the idea that brought such ecstasy ironically turned to gall and wormwood. *If this was Sally's room, she had moved . . . recently. She was gone.*

Jay could not shake the strange conjecture that Sally had been here. It clung to the lining of his soul like soft lint, refusing to be brushed off.

The boarding house "family" whispered theories about its new occupant. The female population speculated at length on the "business" of the new, handsome "eligible" within their walls. Each eyed him as a matrimonial prospect for her daughter, granddaughter, niece, or sister. His friendly manner and ready smile brought worshipful glances at the dining table. And when he arose from his meal to help Mrs. Gordon clear the table, heads turned fast enough to send hairpins flying. Here was an unusual breed.

Besides being instinctively helpful, however, Jay had ulterior motives for his generous expenditure of time. He wished to learn if Sally ever roomed in this inn.

"It's a pity the pretty little cook wasn't still here, Annabelle," an arthritic roomer said in a stage whisper. "Wouldn't she and the new boarder a' made a fetching match, though?"

Jay heard but ignored the comments, his mind bent on a singular goal. To everyone's astonishment, he helped the dour Mrs. Gordon with the dishes, hauling out her pans of oily dishwater and scrubbing the scullery floor, causing one eagle-eyed maiden to ask, "She ain't *hired* him on, has she?"

"Let's sit and visit over a good cup of coffee," Jay suggested when the work was done two hours ahead of schedule. "I need to ask some questions in connection with my . . . business here."

"I'll help all I can."

Pools of sweat accumulated on Mrs. Gordon's fleshy face; her round cheeks radiated heat. "Your room suitable?" He detected a hint of hopefulness in her tired voice.

"I believe you gave me a *girl's* room," he teased.

"I'll put you someplace else if you want. I'll have someone change with you . . ."

"No, no. The room is fine. But a girl did stay there before I came, didn't she?"

"Yes. How did you know?"

"I can *smell* a girl's room for a mile!" He said it lightly, playfully.

"I . . . scoured it . . ."

"Girls don't bother me. I lived with my grandmother as the only man in the house for years. I was just wondering what the girl before me was like. Partly curiosity."

"She kept a clean room."

"I meant . . ."

"She was my cook."

"Oh, I see . . ." Jay's voice showed unintentional disappointment.

"Ran out on me when I needed her the worst."

Couldn't have been Sally.

"She had long, shaggy hair that I had to threaten to cut off mannish because she wouldn't take care of it while she waited the kitchen . . ."

Couldn't have been Sally.

169

"She was a good enough cook, but lazy. She played sick half the time, throwing me into all sorts of hardships to get a meal on a minute's notice. I didn't like the way she dressed, either. She had one old slouchy yellow-colored dress with hanging sleeves that she wore constantly. I never learned what she did with the whole duffle bag of nice clothing she brought with her when she came . . ."

Couldn't have been Sally.

"She came to me a homeless waif, near penniless. She'd play off her work, then expect me to cotton to her needs when I already had my hands full. She even played me against my boarders . . ." Mrs. Gordon's bottled-up resentment, born of jealousy, rolled out.

Couldn't have been Sally.

"I had a special customer, big shot with the telephone company, and she buttered up to him for the tips he always left me, and she actually tried to steal the money he left on his dinner tray. Fortunately I caught her at her own game before she stole me blind."

Couldn't have been Sally. Aloud he said, "What was her name, Mrs. Gordon?"

"Her name was Harriet. Miss Harriet. But the one thing she did was keep a clean room."

Thank God, it wasn't Sally! "Did you ever have a boarder by the name of Sally Harris?"

"No, I never heard that name, and I'm good at remembering every name and face that occupies a room even for a night. What did she look like?"

"She was tiny-waisted with long, golden hair and eyes the color of bluebonnet flowers in the springtime. Her face was pure as a lily and fresh without help. She had a brown travel bag and a small velvet purse."

Mrs. Gordon narrowed her eyes and looked away, giving the impression that Jay had hit on a raw nerve in her memory. "I said I never had a Sally Harris rooming here," she repeated, a bit too firmly.

Jay began his search, but at the end of the week he had found no further clues. His checklist included parsons, schoolteachers, storekeepers and bystanders.

Still, varied disclosures that the regular boarding house tenents gave of the recent "cook" perplexed him. Some of them drew word pictures of Sally, while common sense and Mrs. Gordon's contradictory remarks about the "selfish, thoughtless" girl who "deserted her" in a lurch could bear no resemblance to the sweet vision of womanhood Jay held in his heart of Sally Harris. So eventually he ruled out Sally Harris as ever setting foot in Mrs. Gordon's house. Despite his intuition, she had never occupied his room, he told himself.

Quite by accident, Jay met Nurse Banks as she came to administer medicine to an old patient and friend of hers at the boarding house. The same longsuffering, mother kindness that had drawn Sally into her confidence reached out to Jay. He found himself conversing with her easily.

"You must get around a lot in this town," he commented.

"Very few here I don't know by first name," she admitted with a proud sort of humility.

"Maybe you can help me, then," he told her. "I'm on an important errand. I'm looking for a friend who left home a few weeks ago and apparently came here."

"What is his name?"

Jay smiled. "The person I'm looking for is a young lady. Her name is Sally Harris. I don't suppose that you have met her?"

Nurse Banks hesitated; Jay felt that she searched his soul. "Yes, I've seen her. Long golden hair. Blue eyes . . ."

Jay lurched. "Where did you see her?"

"I told her I would not tell."

"But . . . can't you tell me *anything?*"

The nurse's eyes twinkled. "Actually, I told her I would use my own good judgment about giving out information. I have a premonition she wouldn't care if I told the handsome prince who seems to care so much!"

"I'll take all the blame for your broken promises."

"When I saw her, she lived right here."

"Where did she go from here?"

"She went home. She was recovering from an illness when I met her. It was mostly homesickness, I think. She said as soon as she was able to be up and travel she was going to board the westbound train and return to her home. I told her that was the best thing she could do and wished her luck. I got tied up with a case and haven't been back since she left."

"How . . . long ago was that?"

"Oh, it's been quite a spell ago. Several weeks. I'm sure she's been home long since! You'd best check there. She's probably pressing her cheek on the windowpane watching for you right now."

Jay groaned. "Miss Banks, Sally never made it home."

Chapter Twenty-One

The Ghost

"*L*ook! Yonder's th' goody-goody." Monroe punched his reckless friend, Sarge. "What'ya say he's still lookin' for our mermaid?"

"If he *does* find her, he'll be an easy one to take her away from. And I won't mind a-doin' it. Remember, Monroe, *we* found her first. She's rightly ours. We might do ourselves a favor to inform him of that, too."

"The chap may be stronger than he looks. He sure had those fists clinched when he left t'other day."

"Just so he don't find the girl on a weekend. I'm no 'count on weekends."

"What can you 'spect, stayin' out all night and noonin' in for grub?"

"Shhh. He's comin' this direction. If I start up some fun, don't you spoil it, d'ya hear?" Monroe and Sarge pretended to study the distant horizon.

"Hello, gentlemen." The two turned, fabricating a look of innocence.

"Why, howdy, mister. Found your Lady Goldilocks yet?" Monroe asked amicably.

"No." The one word, framed in pained silence, seemed suspended while Jay hunted for his voice to continue. "Have you . . . seen her? Did she . . . go back down the river?"

Monroe gave Sarge a slow, wicked wink. "She's been comin' down to the river bank just after dark each night for the past week or so in a sort of glowing-like garb. We can't quite figure what she's doing, though."

"Nope, we can't figure her out," chimed in Sarge.

"You've actually seen her? She . . . she comes *here?*" Jay shook his head in blissful disbelief.

"Indeed she does. But when we try to capture her, she just disappears. We think it might be her ghost."

"I'm sure . . . it isn't a spirit."

"Don't you believe in ghosts, mister?"

"No."

"Then why don't you come and see for yourself tonight? I dare say, she'll be back to attend to her business."

"What does she do when she comes to the water?"

Monroe hunched his shoulders. "As far as we can tell, she just mumbles something."

"And you forgot, Monroe, she drops the glisteny things into the very edge of the water."

"I almost forgot to tell him that, Sarge. Thank you for reminding me. That might be important. Does any of this make any sense to you, sir?"

"No. Show me where she stands."

Monroe backed up, cocked his head to one side, seemed to measure distance in his mind, and imperceptibly dropped the lid of his right eye again. "Where would you say she stands *exactly*, Sarge?"

"Right there where the gent is standing now."

"There's . . . no footprints of a lady."

"We told you, mister, that it's her ghost that's hainting the river at night. Ghosts don't make no footprints."

Jay knelt and peered into the water, feeling along the silt-bottom riverbed with both his hands, while the prevaricators struggled to keep a sober countenance. Finding nothing, Jay arose and wiped his hands on his shirt. "Thank you for telling me," he said.

"You'll be here tonight to see for yourself?"

"I'll be here."

"I think we ought to tell you that she doesn't stay long, mister. You don't want to miss her."

"No, I . . . can't miss her." Some of the tortured expression left Jay's face. "If she comes tonight, I'll see her." He turned and left.

"Now what we gonna do with him when he comes tonight, Monroe?"

"Leave that to me."

"I know you got a plan, so out with it. We're gonna have some fun, ain't we?"

"Yeah. I was thinkin' on havin' you dress up like a girl ghost and stand by the river and . . ."

"*You* should be the ghost. You're the one that did sech a perty modelin' job in her blue dress at th' bar, remember?"

"Whichever it is of us that is the haint has got to grab him when he comes near."

"Where'll we get the ghost rags?"

"We'll take a bleached domestic sheet off'n a clothes-line around here somewhere."

"If you had stayed with your old lady, we could have borrowed one from her."

"If I had stayed with my old lady, she wouldn't'a let me out of the house to have so much fun tonight."

"What are we gonna do with goody-goody when we capture him?"

"Show him how much we love and respect goody-goodies here in this rip-roarin' place. He'll think he met up with a cross between a curly wolf and a swamp alligator when he goes back to town a-mermaid huntin'. *If* he goes back alive . . ."

A cloud of uneasiness built to storm porportions inside Jay just before dinner was served. Even praying failed to dissolve its violence. He scarcely touched his food, hoping that Mrs. Gordon would not notice.

Wishing to be completely honest with the landlady, yet not wanting to divulge his business to her, he said, "Mrs. Gordon, I will probably not be in by curfew tonight." He helped her scrape the plates into the slop bucket.

"You're not starting to . . . break my rules? Because if you are . . ."

"No, ma'am. I have a bit of business to attend that will take me . . . away until . . . late. I just wanted you to know so that you would not worry when I did not return."

"And what time will your business be completed? I can leave the door unlatched an extra half hour."

Jay sighed. "I do wish I could tell you, Mrs. Gordon.

But unfortunately, the nature of my business is such that perhaps I should plan to . . . lodge elsewhere tonight so as not to bother you."

"Very well. I will wait until half past to bolt the door. But not one minute longer."

"Thank you."

It won't be the first time I've slept under the stars, Jay mused, leaning his head against the window sill and letting his mind plunge back to the lonely days when he and Patches roamed homelessly. Had that been only a few short months ago? It seemed an eternity.

Jay turned from the window and pulled the sheet from his bed, rolling it into a tight ball. If sleeping in the woods tonight should fall his lot, the coverlet would protect him from the merciless mosquitoes that swarmed in maddening droves along the waterfront.

The clock thumped out six measured gongs. Mrs. Gordon would still be in the kitchen, and if Jay hurried she would not see the bundle he carried, sparing him an interrogation. Just to be on his way, entertaining a slim hope that he might see Sally this very night, should have lifted his spirits. But heaviness still clothed his soul like iron armor.

Had Jay's senses been tuned to nature's symphony, the walk to the river would have been quite pleasant. Rangy dandelions, no longer vain about their beauty, headed out to cottony spores that listed away from late summer's hot breath. Bois d'arc apples littered the ground under twisted parent trees.

Dancing their silhouettes along the narrow lane, an arpeggio of sheeny black starlings pecked away with bobbing beaks. The path, a quagmire of mud when it rained, was now paved with powdery dust.

Permeating the air was a blend of smells—sweet honeysuckle, mildewed broomweed, and the fishy odor of water-sogged docks.

Jay saw and smelled and felt without conscious comprehension and presently found himself at the appointed place. He skirted the spot pointed out by the two river men and located a shady haven protected by a large, low-hanging salt cedar. Within a few minutes, his body, fatigued by worry and tension, slumped into a flighty sleep.

Voices—men's voices—awoke him. The sun had set and only a trace of light now remained to link evening with night. "I don't believe he's here yet, Monroe."

"Nope, don't seem so."

"Do you think he'll come?"

"Yep. Thinks too much of that girl not to come. He should be right along. We sure put one over on him. He never suspicioned a thing. I could see in his eyes he didn't."

"You're just *too* good, Monroe!" Sarge slapped his knee in an exaggerated fit of laughter.

"Now get you on that garb and get down by the river . . ."

"And what if he puts up a ruckus when I try to grab him?"

"I'll be here to help, stupid. Both of us together ought to be able to drown one unarmed man. If we can't do that little job, it's *us* that ought to be drowned . . ."

Confused, Jay felt his heart drop to a new low of despair. Not because he feared what the two rogues might do to him, but because he now realized their story was but a cruel hoax. He would not find Sally at the river tonight!

Even with disappointment biting into his mind like a crosscut saw, Jay quickly devised a plan to escape his tormentors. Mindful to thank God for the disclosure, he slowly unrolled the knotted sheet, taking care to make no noise. The sound of rushing water gave him an advantage. Then with the sheet over his body, he moved from his hiding place toward the river bank, slowly waving his arms and moaning.

"Monroe!" shrieked Sarge, grappling wildly for the larger man. "Here she comes!"

"Run, Sarge, run!" bellowed Monroe, leaving the unfortunate man to stumble, fall, rise and trip again over his clumsy garb.

"Wait on me, Monroe! Please don't leave me here with the ghost! This was your idea. You promised, Monroe. O-o-o-o-o-o . . ."

Sarge hit the ground with a heavy thud; he had fainted.

Jay rushed forward to make apologies and help the man up, but Monroe flew at him in a frenzied rage. "Mermaid lady! You go away! You've given us enough trouble already. If you'll leave us alone, we'll leave you alone. We promise! I'll see after my friend myself. Go away! Shoooooo, do you hear?" Monroe waved his brawny arms toward Jay.

Fearful that Monroe might pass out too, Jay made his way back toward town. He took off the sheet and rolled it into a ball again. At any other time, the irony of the night would have brought a smile to his lips. But how could he ever smile again until he found Sally?

179

Back at the boarding house he found that Mrs. Gordon had not locked the door yet.

Chapter Twenty-Two

A New Danger

*"G*ood morning, beautiful Miss Harriet . . ."

The telephone exchange where Sally worked lay across the river from Fort Fisher in a booming suburb called Pleasant Valley, itself an annex of Waco. The subdivision was perhaps no less brawling than its neighbors but situated farther from the raw river front and thus more sophisticated.

Sally possessed a classic beauty—or vice versa—that could not be hidden for long in a growing metropolis. The first to respond overtly to her charms, claiming them for himself, was a disreputable lineman named Eli Adams whose employment with her company brought him to the office where she worked. Rumor had it that this young man was divorced, but Sally was not a part of the rumor mill, and Eli hid his past well when he wished.

Eli's petty talk and constant show of attention,

bordering the ridiculous, irritated Sally at first, then flattered her. Why should she not be included in the world about her? Was this not what she had sought when she left the stagnation of farm life?

Fast and reckless, Eli knew the way to awaken a maiden's vanity and soon had Sally glancing self-consciously in the powder room mirror at her flawless face during each break.

His next move was to ask to escort her to dinner "in town." Unfortunately, the invitation came while Mr. Cotterby was away. The only other person to whom Sally could go for advice was Mrs. Mason, and that naive lady could only draw her conclusions of the young man's character from Sally's inaccurate accounts. So a date was set.

Mrs. Mason withheld her peace to the last. Then she said, "I'm not your mother, Sally, but I'd like you to be back by dark so that I won't worry about your safety."

"Oh, surely, Mrs. Mason," Sally replied. "Dinner shouldn't take four hours!"

"I . . . do wish I knew a little more about Mr. Adams. I've never heard Seth mention him. But if he works for the company . . . Oh, dear, I wish Seth was here . . ."

"I don't know any better way to learn about a person than to be in his company," laughed Sally, feeling grown up. "And he has assured me that another couple will join us at the restaurant, so we won't be alone."

Mrs. Mason sighed, a mixture of apprehension and relief. "That makes me feel better. It was thoughtful of him to invite another couple. There's safety in numbers, my mother always said."

Sally watched nervously for Eli. She intercepted him

at the door before he could lift the heavy brass knocker
that would apprise the lady of the house of his presence.
She had an intuitive feeling that Mrs. Mason would not
look favorably upon her choice of dinner partner. Then
a new thought startled her. Would God approve? Was Eli
a Christian? Too late, her dawdling conscience reminded
her that she had failed to ask God what His will might
be in the matter. Eli reached for her arm and drew her
toward the street.

Few had been Sally's social engagements, selected
with diligent screening by Martha. Molly's delicious
whispers were Sally's only knowledge of what real
romance might be like. Eli, though, proved a veteran
attendant of ladies, entertaining Sally with his wit and
foolishness, never lacking for words or actions. He guid-
ed her to the car line and hailed a lumbering trolley. Sally
realized she did not even know their destination.

"I . . . hope it isn't dreadfully far to the restaurant,"
Sally said, almost in a whisper.

"What difference should it make?" quipped Eli. "You
have a strong, fearless bodyguard."

"Mrs. Mason wishes me in by dark." Seated beside
this grown man, the words seemed stupidly juvenile—as
if she must be tucked into bed by her landlord at eight
o'clock!

His look of surprise lasted only long enough for the
rumble of mocking laughter to reach the surface of his
swarthy face. "You're with me tonight, beautiful, not the
Mason Jar. The stuffy old gal has had her day; now it's
time for you to have yours. You've been caged up too long
already. I'll take care of you." He chucked her under the
chin.

Sally glanced at him searchingly. He winked mischievously. Of course, he did not mean what he said; he teased carelessly, even at the office. She would have to learn his harmless ways.

"You know, Miss Harriet," he inched his face closer to hers, "I thought perhaps you'd want to wear just a bit of face tint for this special occasion. For evening, you look just a little pale . . ."

Sally pulled away. "I've never worn paint."

"Well, don't fret, beautiful. My buddy will have his lady friend with him tonight, and she'll have some extra face dope. You can take some tips from her. With time, you'll learn the modern ways. You're not a born-and-bred city girl, are you?"

"No."

"I thought not."

Eyes of fellow passengers focused on the closeness of the two and made Sally feel cheap. She sat stiffly, wishing the ride would end.

Eli hurried her from car to cafe, shielding her from the surrounding scenes. Candles flickered in the dim interior of the eatery he chose. Obviously he had patronized the establishment many times before. Gaudily bejeweled waitresses in alluring costume stopped to exchange pleasantries with him.

"Is Jud coming?" a dark, bangled girl asked.

"He wouldn't miss it, darling," Eli answered familiarly. "And we'll wait our meal until he arrives, please."

Conversation between Sally and Eli became even more one-sided as their worlds moved apart; there was little in common to discuss except the telephone company.

In an effort to untie her tongue, Sally asked, "Where

is your next job assignment?'' She was forced to repeat the question to be heard over the noise of shuffling feet on the floor in an adjoining room.

Abstractedly he answered, ''Aw, they're sending me out to the county seat of old Bosque next week.''

Sally's mind reeled into focus, and Eli caught her perceptive movement. ''You know that neck of the woods, beautiful?''

''I've been there . . . when I was a kid'' Sally said.

''I'll headquarter in Meridian. But my work will mostly be in that exploding railroad town.''

''The Springs?''

''I think they call it Walnut Springs. I'll be there and in the outlying areas. We're putting up a lot of new lines in those parts. Population bursting at the seams.'' He paused and reached over to pat her cheek with unrestrained affection. ''Why, beautiful, you're coming out of your shell. You're actually *talking.*''

''It's just that I . . . have a friend that works in The Springs.''

Eli's jaw tightened, his face twisted. ''What's his name?''

Sally laughed, a short, skin-deep sort of laugh that came out too high-pitched. *''Her* name is Molly Rushing. She works as a soda jerk in the drug store there.''

''I'll be happy to look her up and give her your regards.''

It became evident that any talk concerning their jobs bored Eli.

Jud, his countenance atrophied by dissipation, piloted his girl through the smoke-filled room to Eli's table. Sally's unbelieving eyes dropped in shame for the poor girl with

185

bare arms dangling from puffs of thin material that could never be called sleeves. She stifled a desire to share her own scarf with one whose neckline plunged too low to hide her terrible immodesty. Lips and nails seemed to bleed crimson red, while quarter-sized spots of rouge on her cheeks added to the whole clownlike effect. Sally scarcely made it back to rationality in time for the introductions.

"Miss Harriet and I work for the same company," Eli was saying suavely. "She's all new to our world." (He spoke as if to explain Sally's disgraceful plainness.)

The girl whom Jud called Bootsy gave Sally a disdainful look. "Won't take her long to learn if she's worth developing," she quipped, whipping out a cigarette. She leaned forward to light it by the dancing flame of the candle that sat center table. "I'm perishing for a puff."

The world about Sally whirled out of adjustment again. "Bring us something cool to drink," Eli told a passing waitress. "We're thirsty." He grappled at his cheap, ill-knotted necktie, loosening it.

After one taste of the throat-searing liquid, Sally refused the "refreshing" quencher. Confused thoughts churned in her benumbed mind. The chasm between her and the strange man with whom she had promised to dine widened until she wanted to stand on her side of the cliff and protest that the whole unfortunate meeting was a miserable mistake, a cruel joke, a torrid nightmare. Who would find her . . . if . . . her life ended here? Mr. Cotterby was out of town, Mrs. Mason had no idea where she was, and her parents, miles away . . .

Eli's evening had just begun. The more he drank, the more boisterous his language became. When the meal was served, he consumed it ravenously, frequently lifting his glass for a refill. Sally hardly touched her food, the seriousness of her plight digging trenches in her thoughts.

Finally, Bootsy, becoming glassy-eyed herself, motioned for Sally to follow her to the women's room. Sally considered this invitation preferable to staying in the company of the two inebriated men.

Cocooned in the lounge, Bootsy turned on Sally angrily. "Matty said you'd best keep your dirty hands off her Eli. She said . . ."

"Wait a minute, please. I haven't had my hands on Eli, and who is Matty anyway?"

"She's Eli's ex and my best friend!"

"Eli's ex what?"

"Why, ex-wife, of course, stupid. He may have divorced her for a dunce like you, but she still has a claim on him on account of the baby . . ."

"Miss Bootsy, will you please tell Matty that I am in no way a threat to her husband . . ."

"Her *ex* . . ."

". . . her *ex*-husband, and I will promise her, you, myself, and God that if I ever get safely home from this deplorable place, I will never be caught here again . . . or anywhere else in the company of Mr. Eli Adams. I don't *want* him!"

"Look, chick," her blurry eyes strained toward sobriety. "You are too soft and pious to be here anyhow."

"Thank you for the compliment."

Bumping sounds from the closed-off room nearby intensified.

"Are you gonna dansh with him?"

"No!"

"Then scram before *she* gets here to check on him!"

Sally, using all her faculties of good judgment, went directly to the manager and asked directions to a car that would take her back to Pleasant Valley.

"Have you paid for your meal, ma'am?" he asked her bluntly. "We don't let nobody out them doors until they pay their bill."

A panic seized Sally; she had no money. Promises and prayers bumped against each other on their way upward to a merciful God. "I . . ."

"I'll pay her bill, Chuck," a quiet, steady voice said. Sally had not seen the man standing there and wondered if he might be an angel. He pushed a nickel into her hand. "You'll need this for carfare," he said. "You don't belong here." She looked around to thank him, but he was gone.

Sally turned to flee. "Wait, lady," the portly bartender called after her. "Were there drinks?"

"One was ordered for me . . . that I didn't drink." The man gaped after her blankly, his dumb stare asking why she had come to the tavern at all.

With more prayer and more help from strangers (or were they angels?), Sally found her way to the proper car. She dropped into a seat and leaned her tired, spinning head on the window casing, letting the tears fall. What would she tell Mrs. Mason? *I'll tell her the truth . . . and if she no longer wants a girl like me, who disgraced myself by being seen in a tavern, then I'll . . .*she shuddered. *But there'll be no more lies, no more dishonesty, whatever it costs me. God, please let Mrs. Mason keep me until I get my paycheck. Oh, just one more week! If I can work one more week . . .*

The car jostled over an uneven railroad track, past a row of sooty chimneys and gray factories, then into a downtown section. Sally stared out aimlessly.

Faces passed in a blur, all a mass of milling humanity that melted into insignificance. Then a tall young man standing on the boardwalk at a busy intersection arrested her attention. He held his head regally, his character photographed in his fine, firm chin. His face alone stood out from the mob. Self-control and strength of soul showed in the one glimpse she was afforded of his lofty face. How different he was from the weak excuse of manhood whose company she had just departed! Subconsciously, rather than analytically, she labeled him as one who would protect a lady.

For an instant their eyes met, and the gentleman tipped his hat and started as though he would pursue the car and speak to her.

How strange! A sensation that she had met him before gripped Sally. But of course that was impossible. She was a stranger in this place. She accused her fickle emotions of playing pranks on her in a vulnerable moment.

That night she dreamed about the face on the street corner. "Sally!" he called, pleadingly. He reached toward her with his hand. And then he disappeared into the masses.

Chapter Twenty-Three

Frustration

So near and yet so far . . .

Jay tossed on the hard cot, his mind even more restless than his worn body. No one seemed to know a Sally Harris. He had checked at every rooming house, rental agency, school, church, and millinery. Mrs. Gordon still avouched that no Sally Harris had lived there in spite of the nurse's tidings to the contrary. "Miss Banks is mistaken." She set her lips grimly.

Jay had gone from wild peaks of hope to even wilder plunges of despair. And today he was sure that he had seen her on a public conveyance headed for an unknown destination. The face he saw was streaked with tears, ravaged with strain, and . . . desperate. Branded in his memory, it haunted him yet.

If Miss Banks's story was true, Sally had planned to return home several weeks ago. Why hadn't she? Questions outran answers, stripping sleep from Jay's weary eyelids.

The next evening, Mr. Cotterby checked in at Mrs. Gordon's lodge. Jay squandered no time making acquaintance with the dignified-looking gentleman, discovering that he was an executive with the telephone company, in and out of the area as his job dictated.

"So you've stayed here before?" Jay ventured, in anxious politeness, another of his dozens of ways of prefacing his inquisition.

"Oh, yes. Often. This is my home on the road. I've stayed here off and on for a year or more now. I have a widowed sister who lives just across the river in Pleasant Valley, but we both thought it would be best for me to stay here, for the benefit of those tongues who might not know that we are related. When I call to take her to dinner, the neighbors think she has a suitor!"

"This is . . . the most commodious place to room around here?"

"It is. It has its advantages and disadvantages, of course. But it has the others bested a mile. Business picked up here for a few weeks when Mrs. Gordon had the little golden-haired cook. I couldn't have gotten a room myself if I hadn't been a standing customer. There was actually a waiting list. Say, could that girl cook! Never tasted such light breakfast rolls! Old-fashioned *country* cooking!"

"I wish she was still here," Jay laughed. "I could stand a good country meal. What happened to that good cook?"

"I kidnapped her." Mr. Cotterby kept his face straight, but his eyes crinkled in laughter.

"You . . . what?"

He laughed aloud, then sobered to explain. "It really was a sad story," he relayed. "The girl came here from out of nowhere on the mercies of Mrs. Gordon. She had no family, no relatives, precious little money. Mrs. Gordon called her a 'homeless waif' and treated her . . . well, shamefully, really. Made the tiny thing work from before good daylight until after dark—without pay."

"Without pay?"

"Except for room and board. There ought to be a law against it, I say. Working a body that many hours straight. I left the child a dime tip, and the tightfist took it away from her."

"How did you find out?"

"Kept my eyes open. Watched the child get weaker . . . lose her spirit . . . her fight . . . her will to live. She did everything without heart. But, believe me, her cooking—even with no heart—beat the vile grub we get now!"

"How did you get her away?"

"I offered the girl a job with my company, and she took it."

"How nice of you to rescue her."

"Yes. The old termagant was holding the scissors to cut off that beautiful gold hair when I went with her to gather her belongings . . ."

"Where is she now? The girl, I mean."

"She lives across the river with my sister, who is quite struck with her. She went to work for me about two weeks ago, and I've never seen anyone learn faster. I saw right away that I had a genius on my hands. Supervisor material. I'll likely take her down to Austin soon where she can make more money. I'm just back from a business trip, and I haven't approached her about it yet. I hope she'll agree to the transfer. It's quite an opportunity for one so young."

"How old is she?"

"She's suspended between eighteen and nineteen somewhere. Hasn't been graduated from school long."

"What is her name?"

"Harriet. Miss Harriet."

"Oh, yes. Mrs. Gordon told me. You know nothing of her background?"

"No. She went to some obscure rural school, and I sent for her scholastic records, but even they disclaim any knowledge of her."

Jay's hopes toppled, shattered again. The girl Mr. Cotterby described could not be Sally.

"And are you here with your job?" Mr. Cotterby asked in reciprocal interest.

"No. I'm not employed at the present. I'm here on a special mission, looking for a young lady. That was my reason for questioning you so thoroughly."

"Oh, I thought perhaps you were interested romantically," teased Mr. Cotterby.

"I wish my responsibility went no farther than that," admitted Jay.

"I'm sorry that I can be of no assistance," Mr. Cotterby said, and the conversation turned to generalities.

When Seth Cotterby checked in with his sister and Sally the following morning, he sensed a change in Sally. Behind her lovely blue eyes that smiled on the surface lay an unidentified graveness. Mr. Cotterby gave an account of his travels to the extent that he felt would be of interest to the ladies and then mentioned his evening at Mrs. Gordon's famed rooming house. "Perhaps I rescued you too soon," he teased Sally.

"Why, I scarcely escaped with the hair of my head!" she countered.

"But there's a young single man rooming there now that would have been glad to rescue you, I'm sure! And he's worth his salt unless I miss my guess. Fine specimen of a man."

"I've . . . had my fill of men since you've been gone, I'm afraid," Sally answered wryly, casting a sidewise glance at Mrs. Mason. "My social life ended with one bad experience."

"Is the man known to me?" Mr. Cobberby raised his eyebrows, soliciting an answer from first one and then the other.

"Eli Adams."

"You don't mean . . . Has Eli Adams been bothering you, Miss Harriet?" He looked at her as if measuring her sincerity.

"It's over now, Mr. Cotterby. He'll never have the chance to . . . bother me again."

"No, he won't," vowed Seth Cotterby, clamping his lips together. "I should have warned you before I left."

"I shouldn't have tried anything . . . on my own."

"Now I could approve of the one at the boarding house," began Mr. Cotterby. "He's all honesty and integrity, besides being maddeningly handsome. But he's not the least bit interested in romance. He's here searching for a golden-haired lass that he says he saw floating downstream by boat a few weeks ago."

Sally's eyes widened guiltily, though of course the

gentlemen could not have been talking about her. It was simply a coincidence.

"Wouldn't be you he was searching for would it, Miss Harriet?"

"Why . . . no, I don't suppose so. I . . . I'm sure I don't know who it should be that would . . . know I am here . . ."

"A brother, perhaps?"

"No, sir. All my brothers are married except one. And he's military. I'm sure it wouldn't be him."

"You don't know a gentleman, twentyish and handsome, dark hair and eyes, of six-foot frame?"

"No, sir. No one that I know fits that description."

"Too bad. I guess you aren't the one. I had hoped you were."

"Did he give the girl's name?" spoke up Mrs. Mason.

"No. He just said it wasn't Harriet."

"Miss Harriet's name isn't Harriet, Seth. That's why the school couldn't find her records. Her certified name is Sally Harris."

Mr. Cotterby turned to Sally for an explanation, puzzled. "I . . . have a confession to make, Mr. Cotterby. In fact, I have two." Sally opened the pages of her past, laying them in order before her new employer. "I'm sorry," she finished, "for my dishonesty."

"How would you feel about a transfer to Austin, Miss Harris?" he asked, his way of accepting her apologies and forgiving her duplicity.

"I'd like to pray about it if I may, Mr. Cotterby. I'm . . . so new in faith. I've already gotten myself into more than one painful situation by not seeking God's will first. I can scarcely afford another mistake."

After another day of fruitless search, Jay knelt beside his bed to form a supplication, but no words of appeal came. She was here somewhere, this elusive golden-haired girl. God knew where she was.

Even in the face of his grandmother's illness and death, Jay had never faced such frustration. To admit defeat was the coward's way. He determined he would not give up until his last penny was spent, his last ounce of strength gone.

He picked up his Bible. The Old Testament required a life for a life. It would not be beautiful reading for an Israelite who had taken a life, but it was God's divine law. Jay told himself that he had robbed the Harris family of the life of their beloved Effie by his participation in the kidnapping crime more than a decade ago. In return, he would give his life, if necessary, to find the daughter of their old age. Martha's heart was bound up in the child that had floated down the river out of her life. Only when he could take Sally back to Martha's arms would the score be settled—a life for a life—and he could take himself honorably from the scene of his sin to begin anew.

Laying aside the Book, he let his thoughts place Martha and Henry alone at the empty harvest table tonight on the farm—the table that once bore the weight of great iron skillets and heavy brownstone dishes to serve a boisterous dozen. Now the offspring had swarmed away to follow their dreams. Their going made the old home echo emptily. The two grieving parents would be awaiting some word—a call, a letter—from him, hinging their future happiness on the news he gave them.

I must call them tomorrow, he decided, consulting a tattered page of calendar that lay between the pages of his Bible. *I've been gone for two weeks now, and Martha will add me to her worry list. It'll help them just to know that I've seen her face, that she's alive.*

But what if that wasn't Sally I saw?

Chapter Twenty-Four

The Prophetic Game

"You play chess?" Carl Ellis, the new tenant at Mrs. Gordon's boarding house, smiled easily as he moved his queen out of the path of a bishop that threatened to capture her. He played alone, moving pieces for both sides.

Jay watched with fascination. "No, sir. I've never had the leisure. What is the object of the game?"

"To take the king eventually. Each piece has rules to move by. Right now the queen is on the run." Carl laughed. "And she's a hard one to catch. She can move any direction she wishes. Most queens *are* hard to catch, you know."

Yes, I know, sighed Jay inwardly. On the surface, he only nodded.

Jay liked Carl although he sensed something in the young man that disturbed him. Was it immaturity? Weakness? Carelessness? He couldn't quite lay a finger on the problem.

"Would you like for me to teach you to play?" Carl offered congenially. "It's really interesting. You can play the game thousands of times and never play it the same way twice. It's an old game that's been around since the thirteenth century. My grandfather taught me to play it."

"You go ahead, Carl. I . . . hardly think I could keep my mind on any game today."

"You do look washed up. If your job is crowding you, I'd be glad to help. It'll be a week or so before the rest of my crew gets here to start on a school we're to build. I came on ahead to get my bearings. I like to . . . feel at home wherever I go." Carl lowered his voice, looking about to assure himself that Mrs. Gordon was not in earshot. "Is this the best this area has for room and board?"

"So they say," Jay returned. "The telephone executive who takes a room here told me that Mrs. Gordon has just recently lost her cook. He says that before this fabulous cook left, the food was superb."

"It's a far cry from that now. Where did the cook go? We'll follow her!"

"She went to work for the telephone company."

"Cooking?"

"No, she changed her career."

"Rotten luck. I guess we'll have to settle for this inferior gruel. But I meant what I said about helping you with your work. I'm pretty handy at about anything and a quick learner."

"Actually, I'm not working," Jay said, weighing his words carefully. How could he inform Carl Ellis of his mission without seeming preposterous? He was in a place he had never been, looking for a girl he had never spoken to, questioning people he did not know. He admitted even to himself that the prospect was enough to baffle any logical mind. "I'm here . . . looking for someone."

"How exciting! I'd rather search for elusive people than work any day! When do we start?"

"I started two weeks ago," Jay said without smiling. "And I had no assurance that she was still here until last evening. I think—I'm quite sure, in fact—that I saw her on a streetcar across the river from here yesterday."

"*Her?* I see that you are trying to capture the queen, too."

"And I'm afraid she's a hard one to catch."

"It's not a particle of my business, Jay, but my curiosity will never rest until I know just why you are trying so hard to capture this lady. Is she your mother, your sister, or your sweetheart? Does she owe you money, perchance?"

A hint of a smile showed in Jay's eyes. "She's young and beautiful. And she's neither my sister nor my sweetheart. Actually, I've only seen her once before—and that was at a distance."

"Then why the frantic search, pray tell?"

"I owe a debt to her parents, and the only way that I can even make partial payment is to find her and take her home to them."

"Oh, I see. She's a . . . delinquent?"

"A runaway would be the better word."

"Maybe she ran away to get married."

Jay winced. "Her parents don't seem to think so."

"And don't you think that if she wished to return to her parents, she would do so of her own accord?"

"I . . . don't know. There are so many unanswered questions. That's why I must find her and talk to her. If

201

indeed it was Sally that I saw yesterday on the transit, the look on her face was . . . desperate. She had been crying."

"This story . . . and the search intrigues me," Carl admitted, forgetting his unfinished chess game. "I'll gladly help. Can you tell me the girl's name and describe her to me?"

"Her name is Sally Harris. She's between eighteen and nineteen years old. Her long hair resembles spun gold when the sun catches it. Her eyes are the blue of a summer sky. She's not very big, and when I saw her yesterday, she had on a soft, blue dress with a white collar."

"How did you know to come here looking for her?"

"I saw her floating up the Brazos River in a flat-bottom boat the day my dog and I came across the state in search of work. As providence would have it, I ended up working for her old heartbroken father. That's when I learned about her disappearance. I promised him that I would find her if she was anywhere to be found. I followed the river and found two salty dock hands who had seen her. They said she stopped here. I even located her boat. Now I have to find *her*."

"There couldn't be an abundance of such lovely young ladies. However, I saw one yesterday that fits the description exactly."

"Where?" Jay almost jumped from his chair.

"In a most unlikely place. She was in a dark, smoke-filled tavern over in Waco."

"I don't . . . believe she would be apt to patronize a tavern. Her parents are strict prohibitionists."

"The girl I saw would have passed for a pure angel straight from heaven's portals. I don't know why she was in the den. I had gone there to see an old friend, Chuck, who works as a manager there. While I talked with him, the sweet-faced innocent walked up—pale and shaken— and asked Chuck how to get to a car that would take her to Pleasant Valley.

"Chuck was awfully curt with the tender thing; he hasn't much respect for ladyfolks. He demanded to know if she had paid for her meal. I saw the panic in the little thing's eyes, and it about wrenched my heart out. I could see that she wanted out of the joint. So I told Chuck that I would pay for whatever she had ordered. Then I told her kindly that she didn't belong in that atmosphere and pushed a nickel into her hand for carfare to take herself home. She must have been penniless. Her childlike gratitude choked me up so that I stepped behind a door until she was out of sight.

"I'll have to admit that I had gone there thinking I might take a drink myself—sometimes I'm weak like that—but after meeting that angel girl, I couldn't. There was something so . . . holy about her. You don't suppose she might have been your lost Sally, do you?"

"I don't think so, sir. It would certainly be out of character with her to be seen in such a place."

"Then we'll keep looking until we find her." Carl turned back to his chessboard. "I think I'll have this queen in about two more moves. Let's see. Yes, it will probably be the knight that captures her. You wait and see. He can turn corners." He studied his next move for a long time, his chin in his hands.

Jay waited, but failed to be held by Carl's intense concentration. His eyes snagged on the ancient pictures on the wall, which peered from behind grease-coated glass.

Why did boarding houses bother to display religious pictures so out of keeping with the rest of their vapid lobbies? Even their dusty frames admitted their failure to influence the unconcerned patronage. Putting Christ on the wall in an oval frame was certainly no substitute for putting Him in one's heart.

"There! She's mine!" Carl grinned as he picked the chess piece from the board. "The queen is mine! I got her!" To see Carl's enthusiasm, one would suppose that Carl had conquered the whole world.

"Congratulations," Jay said.

"And just like that, you will capture *your* queen, Knight Walls."

Jay hoped Carl's prediction was prophetic.

The Strange Wedding

"*D*o you happen to be Miss Molly Rushing?"

The swarthy man smiled, showing even teeth, his elusive quality adding a certain intrigue that Molly had never learned to resist.

The old wide-pegged oak boards of the drugstore might well have been a dance floor as Molly waltzed her graceful form toward Eli Adams. "I am. May I help you, sir?"

"I have heard say that you make heavenly sodas. I'll try one."

"Where did you hear about my sodas, sir?" Molly made her eyes big, expressive.

"Someone gave me a little hint down river a few miles. In a town called Waco."

"I . . . don't believe I know anyone there?"

"A girl as beautiful as you are has friends everywhere!"

"Of whom are you speaking?"

"A Miss Harriet. I took her to dinner one evening, but she ran out on me before the night even started. A real Puritan sort." He rolled his eyeballs comically.

"I don't believe I know a Miss Harriet . . . and it doesn't sound like she'd be my type."

"She said she went to school with you."

"Can you describe her to me?"

"Yellow-colored hair, blue eyes . . ."

"It sounds like Sally Harris, the Puritan part and all. But Sally doesn't live in Waco. She lives twelve miles from here in Brazos Point."

"Harris . . . Harriet . . . Harris. No, I'm sure it was Harriet. I was feeling kind of . . . funny that night, and I remember thinking: Harri-*et* almost none of her food."

Molly laughed at his witless pun.

"She works at the telephone exchange . . ."

"Oh, it couldn't be Sally Harris, then. She could never get a good job like that. It's rumored that Sally is dead, anyhow."

No grass grew under Eli Adams's feet when it came to flirtatious girls. When Molly mentioned a dance at a nearby guest ranch, Eli was all in favor of joining in and neither knew which invited the other to the affair. Nor did it matter. Molly thought to spite Jay Walls, her supposed groom-to-be, and Eli proposed to show "Miss Harriet" a thing or two.

Their kindred spirits were attracted each to the other, and before the night closed its books on the revelry at the ranch, Molly had told Eli of her whirlwind courtship and "engagement" to the recalcitrant Jay Walls, and Eli had promised to stand in as groom in the event she wished an impromptu wedding. The idea pleased the fickle Molly, and she rushed headlong into frantic wedding preparations.

Word reached Myrt and the parson that Molly's floudering marriage plans had revived and that the wedding was on again. Invitations sped by mouth, and the Harris household was notified of the immediate plans.

"I guess Jay give up 'is huntin' o' our Sally an' come back to Th' Springs to marry Molly after all, Henry," Martha twisted the dish towel into a rope while she gave him the surprising news.

Henry ran a shaking hand through his gray, thinning hair. "Don't sound like somethin' he'd be apt to do, Martha. Nope. Don't sound like Jay a tall. I can't fer th' life o' me figger it. Only reason he'd do it 'twould be fer honor sake. He thought he was bound to foller through with what they pinned on 'im as a promise. It's a dirty, lowdown trick Molly pulled on 'im, I 'low."

"But why do you s'pose he didn't leastwise come by an' see us'ns an 'is little dog, Henry? I heared say th' man Molly is marryin' came in from out o' town sever'l nights past an' has been practically livin' on 'er doorstep since."

"Likely he don't wantta tell us he was obliged to give up lookin' fer Sally jest to come back an' marry Molly. An' b'sides, he knows you wouldn't approve 'o his takin' Molly to wife whate'er th' blackmail. You made that clear afore he left."

"Myrt's jest agloatin', Henry."

"You would be too, if'n you was gettin' Jay fer a son-in-law."

"Hit don't seem fair, Henry."

"Will th' weddin' be right here at our own church?"

"That's what Myrt told me t'day. Molly could keer less where it is. She'd jest as soon go to th' justice. But somehow she made a promise to Myrt on account o' her dead mother. 'Tain't on account o' religion. You can mark that down in yore almanac!"

"Jay'd prob'ly feel more comfort'ble if'n we didn't go to th' weddin', Martha."

"Oh, we'll have to go awright, Henry. We're invited, an' Myrt's insistin' on th' whole church congergation bein' there. We don't want no hurt feelin's . . ."

"Then we'll go."

"Myrt knows I ain't hankerin' fer Jay to marry 'er wild granddaughter, an' she'll ferever lord it over my head that Molly won 'im over my objections."

"It's jest somethin' you'll have to live with, Martha. Where they gonna roost when they marry? Here er in Th' Springs?"

"Neither. He's got 'im a good job goin' with th' phone company since he left us, Myrt says, an' he headquarters somewhere down about Waco. They'll live there. Molly ain't got no hankerin' to live nearby."

"Leastwise we won't have to see Jay's constant day-by-day sufferin'."

"Myrt says he travels about puttin' up new telegraph poles an' stretchin' new lines. That's Myrt's story anyhow," she finished dubiously.

"Molly married to a travelin' man . . .?"

"Hush, Henry. Don't say nuthin' wicked. Jay don't know he can't trust Molly when his back is turned. Poor boy. He's got hisself many a heartache in store, I'm afeared."

"That's funny, Martha. None o' this makes a whit o'

sense. Jay never once mentioned to me workin' fer th' phone company. In fact, he once said he warn't a natur'l rollin' stone an' he didn't want no part o' a travelin' job."

"A body takes what he can git when he has a wife to consider."

"When is this joinin' t'gether takin' place?"

"T'night at seven."

"T'night?"

"You heared me. I said t'night."

"You got my serge suit pressed, Martha?"

"I'm heatin' th' sadiron right now, Henry."

"Wonder why he felt th' urge to rush it up so, Martha? I'm thinkin' that if'n he could'a stalled off till he knowed 'er better, he would'a went to th' fer ends o' th' earth to escape marryin' 'er."

"She knowed that, too, Henry. An' don't you never ferget it. Th' nabbin' is her idee. I can't help b'lievin' Jay's bein' forced into somethin' entirely agin' his wishes."

"Wonder if'n he'll take back Patches?"

"Not with 'im travelin'."

"Fer Molly, I mean."

"Molly hates dogs."

"You know, Martha, I guess I was hopin' . . ."

"What was you hopin', Henry?"

"That we'd git Jay in our fam'ly someday. There was somethin' 'bout Jay real special-like."

"One thing was he shared our religion an' was sech a good Christian. Molly'll see that he fergits 'bout th' Lord with her lust fer dancin' an' worldliness, though."

"Jay will never fergit his God, no matter who he marries. It runs real deep with 'im. He even took his Bible when he went to hunt fer Sally."

"You was really hopin' he'd find Sally an' bring 'er back an' that Sally would fetch 'is heart, now warn't you, Henry?"

"I never told it to myself in them words, Martha, but I . . . guess I was."

"So was myself, Henry."

"It's too late now."

"Do you think you could lag outside th' door an' give Jay one last warnin'?"

"I dunno, Martha. I'd be glad to if'n I thought it would spare 'im."

Dressed in their best, Martha and Henry took themselves to the church at the appointed time to witness the union they dreaded. Henry hung back at the door with ulterior motives in mind while Martha took her way to the front to save their seat. Myrt, her ineffective sheet music upside down on the music rack, appeared thoroughly confused. She whirled about on the revolving music stool. Her first note was a terrible discord. Without looking up, the pastor scrawled notes to himself furiously. No ·one seemed happy about anything.

A tanned man with bold eyes made his way up the aisle as Henry slipped into the pew beside Martha. "I ain't seen Jay yet," he breathed. "Can't find 'im."

"That there's th' best man, I guess," whispered Martha. "Weddin's er differ'nt now'days." The procession had started, and Henry signaled her to silence.

Molly, with her face painted more brashly than ever before, floated up the aisle and clasped the hand of the stranger. The whole of the ceremony passed before the disoriented Martha before she knew it had begun. She watched the back door nervously for Jay to make his appearance, even though Molly did not seem concerned whether he showed up or not.

When the pronouncing of man and wife took place, she turned her head from side to side to find the groom, but he was not in evidence. "Where's Jay?" she mouthed to Henry. He shrugged and shook his head.

Martha came near to making an unforgivable social blunder by arising to ask Myrt where the groom was, when the parson turned to the stilled audience. "May I present the new bride and groom to you, ladies and gentlemen: Mr. and Mrs. Eli Adams." He smiled a sickly smile that showed he was only too glad to have the unwelcome job over with.

"Eli Adams?" Martha mumbled, still rattled. "Why, Henry, where's . . .?"

"Sh," warned Henry. "Martha, *she didn't marry Jay!*"

Martha caught at Henry's sleeve. "Let's git ourselves home, Henry," she said weakly. "I'm gettin' swimmy-headed."

Henry half-dragged, half-carried her home. Burden by burden, the scales began to tip against her. The shock of Sally's leaving, the "news" of her possible death, Jay's departure, Molly's sudden wedding to a perfect stranger, and then the overdue demise of Bossy, the family's crippled and aging cow, brought Martha to emotional prostration.

She took to her bed, and Henry called for the doctor, his second experience with the talking machine.

Chapter Twenty-Six

Long-Distance Call

"*L*ong distance, please." Jay held the earpiece clumsily and talked into the protruding horn on the wooden box in front of him.

A pleasing voice came on the line. "May I help you?" Sally's happiness reflected in her sunny response. Tomorrow was payday. She had written her letter and backed it to the Brazos Point destination, and it awaited the purchase of a postage stamp. The joy she felt reverberated through the wires to her customers. It reached to Jay.

"Yes, ma'am. I would like to place a call to a Mr. Henry Harris at Brazos Point . . ."

Sally gasped. "But sir, he doesn't have a . . ."

Jay continued. "The number is 58-J, ma'am. It's a new listing."

Sally, swaying with the shock of being asked to put through a call to her own family, willed her hands to make the connection and ring the number. Her heart stood still when her father answered in his deep, rich dialect.

"Go ahead, please," she advised Jay in a choking tone, but she found that she could not disengage herself from the conversation on the wire.

"Mr. Harris?"

"Yes?"

"This is Jay."

"Jay!" the tired voice sprang to life. "Where are you, Jay?"

"I'm at Fort Fisher, sir, on the Brazos River. I thought I'd best check in lest you worry . . ."

"Have you learned anything?" They were eager words.

"Yes, I found the boat. She came in William's boat. I know she's here somewhere. I've seen her once. I know she's alive, Mr. Harris."

Only by great restraint could Sally keep from shouting her identity over the wires, asking her father to come for her at once. Her soul yearned to run into the arms of the one whose voice now fell in waves of sweet music on her thirsting heart. But to break into another man's conversation would not be ethical.

If only she could say a very few words at the end of the gentleman's conversation! It would tear her heart from her body if she could not speak a word to her precious father!

". . . find Sally soon or it may be too late," the voice of Henry broke into her thoughts. "Her mother is very ill. The doctor came this morning and said . . ."

Sally, hearing mention of her mother's illness, could bear no more. She passed quietly into unconsciousness and heard nothing further.

Jay found to his dismay that he had been disconnected from his party. A series of cracks and a momentary tumult usurped the telephone lines, and then another voice—different from the one that placed his call—broke in: "I'm sorry for the delay, sir. We've had a small problem. We will connect you back with your party at no extra charge." This second voice lacked the softness and sweetness of the original.

Jay talked on another minute, suggesting that Henry remind his wife daily that he would be returning with Sally. "I'm praying it will be any day now," he finished.

Sally lay on the floor in a crumpled heap. When wet compresses failed to rally her, someone sent for Mr. Cotterby, who happened to be in the building. "What happened?" he questioned the other employees.

"She was putting through a call—and just went out all of a sudden," he was informed. He gathered her into his arms and took her to his sister.

"Her system has been through a lot of shocks lately, Seth," Mrs. Mason said as she loosened Sally's sash and removed her button shoes. "A body can just stand so much, and then it collapses."

"I don't want the child worrying about the telephone company or her job for a minute, Sis," Mr. Cotterby declared. "Jobs come and go. Workers come and go. But this girl is special. She's one of a kind—too good to be alone in life, working for the telephone company to survive. She needs to be in a little starched apron in a tiny cottage being taken care of by someone who really loves her. This isn't the life for her . . ."

"I wish I knew how to get in touch with her family."

215

"She told me once that they live in the country and have no telephone."

"Do you think I should call a nurse?"

"I think so. She probably needs rest medicine. I'll pay for whatever she needs."

Sally slept on through the afternoon. Mr. Cotterby looked on anxiously. "Do you think she'll be all right, Sis?"

"I think so, Seth. Her pulse is regular, her breathing normal. I'd say what she has needed for a long time is a good rest."

Mr. Cotterby left for his room at Mrs. Gordon's just before lamp-lighting time, giving instructions that Mrs. Mason should call him if Sally worsened or roused and called for him.

In the parlor of the inn, where threadbare cloaks and slickers hung on the crowded coat rack year around, Mr. Cotterby met up with Jay. "Coming or going?" he asked the young man.

"Going." Jay's steps lagged.

"This late?"

"Yes. I'm going down to Butch's Bar for a minute." He gritted his teeth together.

Mr. Cotterby, misunderstanding, reached out a fatherly hand to detain Jay. "Now look, son, it isn't that bad. Don't give up. You can't lower yourself to that kind of life. It won't help anything . . ."

"I'd do anything to keep from darkening the doors of that devilish place, Mr. Cotterby," Jay's expression carried the anguish he felt. "It's only as a last resort that I go there."

"Don't go . . ." repeated Mr. Cotterby, pleading now.

"A couple of dock tramps told me that *her* gripcase

216

was down there in that den behind the counter, and I thought I might get another clue from . . . them." Uttering the words aloud hurt Jay.

"Then let me go with you."

"Would you?"

"My sister has a sick girl over at her place," Mr. Cotterby said as he measured his pace to Jay's. "That's why I was late getting in. She collapsed this morning at the telephone company."

"I . . . about what time was that?"

"This morning around nine o'clock."

"Strange. I was making a call about that time and my call was interrupted . . ."

"The other employees said she was helping someone put through a call when she blacked out. Might have been yours."

They walked in silence for a block. "But you did get your call through, didn't you, Mr. Walls?"

"Yes. It was *her* parents I was calling. I learned that her mother is very ill. From worry, I'm sure. It's so frustrating not being able to find her, knowing she's here somewhere."

"I don't believe you have ever told me the name of the young lady you are searching for."

"Sally."

"Sally who?"

"Sally Harris."

The name—the truth—the revelation—it all unfolded to Mr. Cotterby like a bone snapped into joint, righting the entire body and relieving all its pain.

"Mr. Walls!" he stopped and caught Jay's arm. "Stop! Sally Harris is at my sister's house!"

Jay, intent on getting to Butch's Bar, failed to comprehend the import of Mr. Cotterby's statement and started on. "But I'm talking about Sally Harris," he said illogically.

"I am, too!"

Jay halted, bewilderd, his mind and Mr. Cotterby's words colliding. "Sally Harris—*my* Sally Harris—is at your sister's house . . . *now?*"

"I'm sure we've found her. The stories match up."

"When . . . how did you find her?"

"She's been found all the time. Sally Harris is the Miss Harriet that cooked for Mrs. Gordon here at the inn."

"But the way Mrs. Gordon described Sally, it couldn't have been . . ."

"You must remember, Mr. Walls, that Mrs. Gordon uses her own particular paintbrush to color things. She was jealous of Sally and her evaluation of the girl bears no resemblance of the real person."

"All the while I've been looking over . . .?"

"Yes, all the while."

"Sally is the girl that Mrs. Gordon almost . . ."

"Scalped!" Mr. Cotterby laughed.

"That beautiful hair!" Jay said it without thought.

"She doesn't know you are looking for her?"

"No. Is she . . . very ill?"

"My sister called a nurse, and the nurse gave her some rest medicine and said she should be better right away."

"How soon?"

"Tonight, I hope. I left word for my sister to call if any changes developed."

"Mr. Cotterby, she *has* to get well—soon."

218

"I'm sure she will. She hasn't had an exactly easy life here, you know. She was fatigued when I found her, and then she adamantly insisted on going right to work for our company so she could pay her own way at my sister's. I suggested she rest a few days, but she would hear none of it."

"I wonder why she didn't at least post a letter to her parents?"

"I couldn't answer that, Mr. Walls. But I can assure you that she is sensitive to the feelings of others, and she must have had her reasons."

"When . . . when can I see her?"

"She's asleep now. We'll have to wait until tomorrow."

"Of course."

Mrs. Gordon stood ready to bolt the door. The tilt of her head as Jay and Mr. Cotterby arrived out of the night labeled them as lawbreakers.

Jay fully expected sleep to desert him, but with the end of his long mission in sight, his body took advantage of the mental respite and sank into a depth of sleep he had not experienced since he left the Harris farm. He overslept breakfast, emerging drugged and drowsy from the hard sleep. He hurried to Mr. Cotterby's quarters, but his friend was out and gone.

In the kitchen, he found Mrs. Gordon sullen and ill-tempered. When Jay asked if Mr. Cotterby had left a message for him, she snapped out Mrs. Mason's address grudgingly. Jay supposed she had never quite forgiven the telephone executive for "stealing" her slave.

Fall just hinted at a cooling surprise with its midmorning air. Jay paused on the river bridge and looked into the clear ripples below, watching a brace of wild ducks wing over the water. Near a bridge, he had first seen her, looking like an angel lost from the massive heavenly host. So small, so alone. He enjoyed thinking she needed him then; he wished she could be his to protect and care for. Now he thought differently.

Yes, she needed him now to get her back to the saftey of her childhood home. But she could never be his. He had murdered her foster sister, brought untold grief to her family, then got himself caught up in a web of romance with a girl she went to school with who would surely step in and hold him to a loveless "promise" he doubted he ever made. No, life had not favored him with the chance to ever call Sally his own.

With trepidation, he lifted the door knocker that would gain him entrance into her presence. Mrs. Mason, like a fairy grown old before her time, flitted to the door, drawing him into the receiving room where Sally sat.

"You have a visitor, Miss Harris. Mr. Jay Walls is here to see you."

Almost he stepped back in dismay when he saw her frailty. The burnished hair, illuminated by the glow of sunbeams streaming in at the east window and brushed into fluffy curls, hung to her slender waist. *And to think that anyone would want to rob her of that hair!*

She lifted long, feathery lashes, looking at him with no sign of recognition, then dropped her eyes shyly. "I don't believe we've met, Mrs. Mason."

"Let me introduce myself, Miss Harris," Jay spoke gently, proceeding with caution. He hardly knew how to say what he wanted to say or exactly what he did intend to say. He had forgotten to prepare a "speech."

Doubt momentarily slipped a cog in Jay's mental wheel. *What if Sally doesn't want to return home? What if she eludes me again? Had she wished to return to the farm, she would surely have sent some word before now.*

"I've seen you, but you've probably not seen me," Jay said, after explaining briefly who he was.

"At the office perhaps?" Her voice was a weak whisper.

"No. The first time I saw you, you were in a small boat floating down the river. Near a railroad bridge. You may have seen my dog . . ."

Sally moved her lips, with deliberate effort, into a patient little smile. "I do remember seeing a spotted dog."

"That was Patches."

"But . . . I didn't see anyone."

"No, I stayed out of sight. I didn't want to . . . frighten you. The other time I saw you was on the streetcar. I was standing at the intersection by the curb."

Sally remembered the terrible night, Eli Adams, and the dream. "Yes . . . I remember."

"I've been looking for you for two weeks."

"Why?"

"I promised your mother and father that I would try to find you and see if you wanted to return to Brazos Point."

"Oh . . ." Tears built in her eyes. "Where . . . did you see my family?"

"I lived with them."

"You did?"

"I think I must have arrived the day after you left. I got . . . stranded there, and I helped your father with the farm work. A terrible rumor spread that you were dead . . ."

221

"Mother thinks I'm *dead?*"

"Not now. I talked with your father on the telephone yesterday . . ."

"It was you! I . . . was your operator . . . and I fainted during the call. I . . . was it a bad dream, or is my mother really sick?" A flicker of concern riddled her eyes.

"She's not doing very well, I'm afraid, Sally." He called her name without forethought. "But it's mostly worry. When we get back to her, she'll get well. Are you ready to go home?"

It was the first spark of life he had seen in her eyes. "Oh, yes! Are you sure . . . mother is going to be all right?"

"We're going to see about her. We'll travel by train as soon as you are able . . ."

"But my job . . ."

Here Mrs. Mason stepped into the conversation. "Seth says you are not to worry about the job for a minute, Sally."

Sally looked at Mrs. Mason, perplexed. "I . . . can go?"

"You are free to go anytime."

"Then I'm able now!" Her cheeks turned rosy with eager anticipation. "Let's . . . surprise them." The nurse caught Mrs. Mason's attention and nodded her head, apparently satisfied.

Mr. Cotterby stepped in from the foyer. Sally looked from Jay to him and back again. "Is . . . he all right to go on a journey with, Mr. Cotterby?" A half-smile pulled at her lips.

"I'd trust Mr. Walls with my own daughter if I had one, but I don't know if I would advise Mr. Walls to trust you." He winked at Jay.

Sally saw the wink but failed to interpret the joke. "What do you mean, Mr. Cotterby?" she asked.

"The last one you took yourself out with got himself married on the rebound."

"Mr. Adams? Married?"

"He came in this morning and announced that he had taken himself a wife. Found her on one of his line jobs, west of here somewhere. Of course, he already had one broken marriage to his credit, and likely as not there'll be another . . ."

Jay listened, not comprehending; somehow Sally felt he needed an explanation. "He's talking about the terrible man I was running away from when you saw me on the streetcar. I said I'd never trust another man. But you're . . . different." Her genuine smile strengthened Jay's heart and weakened his knees.

"Take her home, boy." Mr. Cotterby patted Jay's shoulder. "She doesn't belong in a strange city with the telephone company. She was meant to be a bread baker, not a breadwinner."

The unstamped letter that lay in Sally's lap caught Jay's attention. It was addressed to Henry and Martha Harris. Along with it was the uncashed check from the telephone company. Then he knew.

Chapter Twenty-Seven

Bittersweet Journey

*T*he train heaved and coughed, spitting black phlegm and shaking its internal organs all the way to its red caboose. Jay, adept at making an invalid easy through his many years of caring for his failing grandmother, adjusted Sally's pillow in the car's narrow chair.

"There, are you comfortable now?" He thrilled at her nearness.

"Yes, thank you, Mr. Walls." Her pure blue eyes showed her gratitude.

"I've got to get you home in good shape."

"I . . . don't understand why you are doing this for me . . . and my family. You—a stranger."

"Really, I'm not doing it for you and your family . . . altogether. I have two motives—and I'm afraid both would fall under the heading of selfishness. I'm doing this for . . . me."

225

"Is there . . . a reward for my return?"

"Just a personal reward . . . for my own conscience."

"Your conscience?"

"Yes. Once I committed a terrible crime. The wrong
that I did resulted in a life being lost and a family being
thrown into deep sorrow. When I saw your parents sor-
rowing for you, I thought that if I could find you and erase
that grief it would in some way repay society for the heartache I had caused by my misdeed. Do you understand?"

"I understand. I've . . . got some making up to do,
too. To God and my parents."

"The other reason for my interest was you. When I
first saw you floating down the river, I felt I should . . .
I wanted to . . . make sure you were safe. The world isn't
always a pretty place for an innocent girl."

"What brought you to . . . my parents?"

"Patches and I were left homeless when my grandmother died. She was all the family I had. I started out
too look for work in central Texas where I heard the
railroad had opened up some new shops; I had in mind
a roundhouse job. The railroad pays fair wages. I thought
I might pick up some extra schooling, too.

"Patches and I were following the Brazos River when
my feet got too sore to go on, and we had to lay up. Your
father found us camped down about where you launched
your boat.

"I didn't plan to stay longer than overnight, but your
mother made a big fuss over me, and your father needed
help with the hoeing. They gave me a room . . ."

"Which room is yours?"

Jay turned his attention out the window, centering
it on a streaked longhorn that sparred with a gnarled

stump. "Effie's," he answered, his eyes focusing on the passing landscape, then on nothing at all.

"I'm glad Mama gave you the nicest room. It's the coolest, too, with that big south window."

That south window. One night soon, I'll climb out that south window—the window I crawled in to help commit my crime eleven years ago—and I'll be gone, he promised himself. *I'll leave Sally because my guilt will never let me claim her for my own.*

"One never appreciates home until one is deprived of it," Sally said, a confession rather than an idle statement. "I meant to go back . . . right away."

"Why didn't you?"

"I owed Mrs. Gordon all my money for the rent while I was ill. I couldn't even buy a postage stamp to write home."

"You could have sold biscuits on the side." Jay grinned at her surprise. "Mr. Cotterby would have paid two bits apiece for them. He says you make the world's most wonderful bread."

Sally laughed, a happy, bubbling laugh that struck the tines of Jay's heart and set them vibrating. "Mr. Cotterby just might be prejudiced."

"I'd really like to judge for myself. Do you suppose you could make up a recipe of those rolls for me to sample before I have to leave?"

"Before you . . . *leave?*" An inflection on the last word, suggesting disappointment, pleased Jay more than he cared to acknowledge. "Are you . . . leaving?"

"I'm afraid I must."

"But you've just found me, and . . ." Sally stopped, blushed a pretty pink, caught in the web of her own words and finding no way to advance or retreat.

"My work is complete. Now I can go . . ." Jay started to say "happily," but that would have been a lie, so he substituted "honorably."

"Couldn't you find work at the railroad shops in The Springs . . . and be close by to . . . visit us?"

The train slowed and jerked, its metal cars recoiling at every coupling and setting up a chain of thundering reverberations; Sally only heard the last of Jay's explanation ". . . if it wasn't for that girl . . ."

So he has a girlfriend, Sally thought, the rapture of the day dying, a shadow blotting out her happiness. Her imagination linked him with a fairy-tale princess from a storybook dressed in the palest of soft, rosy chiffons and endowed with enticing dimples just for him. She closed her eyes as if to shut out the prick of pain but only succeeded in locking it in. She felt slightly sick. *The story of my life! The curse of the last! All the worthy young men are taken! But I'll submit to my parents and to God from now on, even if I die a hopeless spinster.*

The train crawled into the station, and Jay hired a phaeton for transportation from the depot to the Harris farm. Each time he solicitiously took her hand to help her in or out, Sally's heart throbbed madly. The touch of his strong hand deepened her love for him, despite her brave efforts to disclaim that love.

Henry had seated Martha in the gently swaying porch swing to savor the mild September day's benediction, when he saw the carriage coming. "I b'lieve we got somebody turnin' into our place, Martha," he said, squinting toward the road and shading his eyes with a weathered hand.

"Who could it be, Henry?" Martha worried anxiously. "Th' house ain't in no shape fer comp'ny. I ain't felt like doin' no bread, y'know."

"Now, don't git in no stew, Martha," he scolded tenderly. "Anybody what knows us knows you been puny. An' if'n it's somebody what don't know us, they won't come in nohow."

"'Tain't one o' th' childern got a new rig, is it, Henry?"

"I don't . . ." The words died on his lips. "Martha! It's our daughter! It's Sally-girl!"

"Is it fer a fact, Henry?" Martha craned her neck to see for herself. "Yes, an' with our Jay, too."

Tears, apologies, love, and gladness mingled to make Sally's homecoming an unforgettable time. Patches brushed a spot bare on the ground with the wagging of his shaggy tail.

On into the late evening, with her motherly prattle Martha slipped Sally back into the world she had once known as if she had never been away. "An' Bossy died whiles you was gone, Sally. Course we was kinda expectin' it, you remember. We shouldn't begrudge 'er th' rest, though, after makin' cream an' butter fer all dozen o' us so faithful. Paw said he'd git us another milker if'n you wanted one . . ."

"An' we got us'ns a gossip machine, Sally," laughed Henry. "Bad as I hate 'um."

"An' we had a weddin' at our church last week." Martha folded her hands in her lap and sat erect for the telling of the important news.

"A wedding? At *our* church in Brazos Point?"

"Guess who."

"I'd never in all the world guess, Mama. I didn't know we had anyone in our church that wasn't married except Widow Myrt," laughed Sally.

"Well, she wasn't 'zactly in our church. She come once in a blue moon. But you got perty close in yer guess. 'Twas Myrt's granddaughter an' yore classmate, Molly."

"Molly Rushing? Molly *married?*" Sally looked to her father for verification; her father watched Jay. Jay, on the verge of a comment, apparently abandoned what he had planned to say and let out his breath slowly, soundlessly.

"Parson Stevens did th' cer'mony. Myrt insisted," Martha explained. " 'Twas a queer cer'mony, too. When we heared it, we thought she was marryin' . . ." Martha held the sentence up in the middle until its significance, and her knowing look, reached Jay. ". . . someone else. A perfect stranger came in, an' I thought shore he was best man. I kept waitin' fer . . ." another look toward Jay ". . . th' groom. An' afore I knowed they'd wed, th' marriage was all over. They ain't aimin' to live here . . ."

"Who did she marry, Mama? One of those wild boys from The Springs that hung out at the drug store?"

"No, he was from out o' country. 'Twas a whirlwind sort o' courtship that shocked ever'body. They said he worked transient puttin' up telegraph poles fer th' phone comp'ny an' was jest passin' through. I heared that on th' party line. You can hear anything. Myrt says it was love at first sight. They lost no time tyin' th' knot."

"Do you remember his name, Mama?"

"Shore do. We was at th' weddin'. Easy name to recall: Eli Adams."

"Eli Adams!" Sally grew pale.

"You knowed him, Sally?"

"I . . . met him once. Molly . . . isn't his first wife."

"She ain't? Oh, Myrt'll *die* when she finds out."

"And Molly probably won't be his last."

"Myrt makes like she's pleased as puddin', but she'd' a heap druther Molly'd married . . . th' other'n." Jay's implication in the story escaped Sally.

"I'm mighty glad she didn't," muttered Jay. Sally was puzzled that the news concerned him at all. Did he know Molly?

"I 'spect you'll have to make th' mornin' bread, Sally. Yore maw ain't been feelin' up to much bakin' lately," Henry said abruptly.

"I've had plenty of practice, Papa. I baked for a whole boarding house where I stayed while I was gone. Anyhow, Mr. Walls has requested a batch of my biscuits before he leaves."

"Afore he *leaves?*" Martha leaned forward in her chair, sputtering objections. "Why, Jay ain't goin' nowhere! He's one o' our'n, Sally!"

Jay hung his head. "I'm afraid I'll have to be moving on now that I've returned your daughter, Mrs. Harris. I couldn't impose on your generosity . . ."

"Oh, stuff an' nonsense," she disputed.

"And I need to get settled into a permanent arrangement before winter."

No more was said, but Martha brought up the subject in the bedchamber while Henry unlaced his hightop shoes. "I had hoped Jay would stay, Henry."

"I had, too, Martha. But things ain't workin' like I'd hoped . . ."

" 'Tween him an' Sally?"

"Yeah."

231

"I can see in 'is eyes that he's mighty fond o' her, Henry, but she keeps 'im at arm's length. Sally is th' beatin'est youngun. I never did understand 'er. Did ya hear 'er call 'im *Mr. Walls*, jest as if'n she ain't accepted 'im as part o' us'ns?"

"I heared all right, Martha. Life's full o' hard games. We can't win 'em all. He brought us back our daughter safe an' sound, an' we can be mighty thankful to th' good Lord fer that. Leastwise we have one."

"D'ya think she'll stay put, Henry?"

"She'll stay put, Martha," he said. "Till she weds."

Led by the Shepherd

Like a shepherd, Thou wilt lead me . . .

The old hymn his grandmother loved came back to support Jay as he rolled his clothing into a small bundle.

The decision to slip out after dark had not been an easy one; it cost bitter pangs. He thrashed it over in his soul, hardly touching the delicious food Sally had prepared for supper. The last meal with the family brought a deep sadness. Sally was especially solicitous, but he couldn't bring himself to meet her eyes. He excused himself early.

He glanced about the room that had been both his torment and his comfort for the fleeting summer months. He longed to leave Sally a note, to tell her how much he loved her, how it hurt to leave her, how lonely his unknown future would be without her. To do so would lessen his pain, but intensify hers. He could never do that.

The half-mast sun hung with lingering appeal, as if

aware that its departure would grant Jay the excuse of darkness he sought in order to make his escape.

Time dragged. Minutes turned to interminable forevers. He vacillated between wanting to coax the clock forward and wanting to hold it back—between wanting to hurry away from her and wanting to linger near her as long as possible. *I'll leave my heart behind,* he told himself, *but my body must go.*

Darkness settled at last. He waited until the lamps went out in the house, then moved noiselessly out the memorable south window and through the yard, giving a low whistle for Patches. He had settled his account as best he could; he was leaving "honorably." The past, present, and future met as friends in the parlor of his soul, understanding and pardoning each other. The strange meeting produced a paradoxical peace.

Near the stalwart oak tree, a sound like a sob caught his attention, and he turned. In the leafy shadows of the monarch stood a lone figure, softly weeping. It was Sally, highlighted by moonbeams that hung in her unbonneted tresses. She lifted tear-filled eyes.

"You are going . . . tonight . . . Jay?" He winced at the caress in her tone as she called his name. *Not Mr. Walls, but Jay!*

"Yes, Sally." There was no way to hide the knapsack. "I . . . must."

She held a small package tied with a ribbon. "Give this to . . . *her.* It's my recipe for the biscuits . . . and a lace kerchief . . . for the wedding. And God's blessings."

"What . . . are you talking about, Sally?"

"The girl . . ."

"What girl?"

"Your . . . sweetheart."

"There's no girl, Sally. I've never had one . . . except you."

"But on the train you said . . ."

"Molly Rushing tried to trick me into marrying her. But that's past, and there was never anything there anyhow."

"You . . . aren't going away to be married?"

"No!"

"Then why are you leaving . . . me?"

"There's something . . . I just must go, Sally."

"Then I'm going, too."

"No, Sally, no!" A terror seized him, clawing at his throat. He could never be guilty of influencing the daughter of Martha and Henry Harris to run away from home a second time. That would add crime to crime.

"Please don't go, Jay."

He felt himself weaken; the debility frightened him. He turned to stumble away quickly while his feet would still cooperate.

"Wait!" she caught his arm, sending a paralyzing thrill all the way to his toes. "You're running from something. Tell me what it is. You can trust me."

"I'm the one that . . . killed Effie." He croaked it out, pulling away.

"You're . . . *what?*"

"I killed an innocent girl. I helped kidnap Effie eleven years ago; helped take her right out that south window there. We bound and gagged her. Laid her on the cold floor of the old barn that burned down."

"Jay! You aren't making sense."

"Sally, I've lived with my crime every minute since

that day. I was only fourteen. Claude was nearly twenty. He promised me big money to help him with a 'cake job.' He caught me at a vulnerable time; I desperately needed money for Grandmother's medicine. I wrote the ransom note and put it on the washstand. I'm as much to blame for Effie's death as Claude is. I've never told anyone . . . who it was that I killed. Your folks don't know that it was . . . Effie. They could never forgive me. You were too young to remember . . ."

"I remember all right. The kidnapping had nothing to do with Effie's death. In fact, Effie didn't even live here when she died. She lived in the Territory of New Mexico with my brother and his wife . . ."

"But she died as a result of the exposure . . . of *pneumonia . . .*"

"I don't know what you're talking about. Effie didn't even have pneumonia!"

"You mean, she didn't die from the wet . . . the cold . . .?"

"Effie died as she would have wanted to die and was buried beside her own mother. We knew—and she knew—that she probably would not live a long life. She went to California to visit her father's grave, and while she was there, she met with an accident that eventually took her."

"Oh, my darling! Say it again! *I* didn't kill Effie? I didn't . . . kill anyone?"

"You didn't." The delightful sound of her soft voice drove the shadows of gloom to the far reaches of eternity. "But you *might* . . . if you go away. I can't . . . live . . . without you, Jay."

"I . . . you . . . my little Sally!" He held out his arms for her eagerly.

Patches sniffed at the package that had fallen heedlessly to the ground, playfully catching the satin ribbon between his teeth, shaking it from side to side.

"You won't . . . leave me?"

"My little Sally! I'll never leave you! I promise!" He pulled her close.

"Thou wilt lead in pastures green . . ."